About Leah Ashton

An unashamed fan of all things happily-ever-after, Leah Ashton has been a lifelong reader of romance. Writing came a little bit later—although in hindsight she's been dreaming up stories for as long as she can remember. Sadly, the most popular boy in school never did suddenly fall head over heels in love with her...

Now she lives in Perth, Western Australia, with her own real-life hero, two gorgeous dogs and the world's smartest cat. By day she works in IT-land; by night she considers herself incredibly lucky to be writing the type of books she loves to read, and to have the opportunity to share her own characters' happily-ever-afters with readers.

You can visit Leah at **www.leah-ashton.com**

Praise for Leah Ashton

'…you've written something both bittersweet and truly moving… Here's a hero who affirms his heroine's completeness, who knows what he's getting into and who tells her that she's all he needs.'
—Dear Author on
Secrets and Speed Dating

'Ashton's debut stands thoroughly apart from its predecessors in both tone and format, and from its opening lines gives plenty of whimsy and quirkiness… Ashton has taken some liberty with the plotting approach and voice of her novel, and this one really stands out as a result.'
—www.readinasinglesitting.com on
Secrets and Speed Dating

'My heart broke for Sophie and her struggles. I really empathised with her character, especially as she is not written as self-pitying or a martyr. She has so much chutzpah and spirit, yet with the perfect amount of pain. Dan is a great hero, too, and brilliantly written; during the major "black moment" I hated and hurt for him at the same time. The premise is original and well developed. I couldn't stop reading as I needed to know how these characters got their HEA. And it's worth it!
—www.everyday-is-the-same.blogspot.co.uk on
Secrets and Speed Dating

Why Resist a Rebel?

Leah Ashton

First published in Great Britain 2013
by Mills & Boon, an imprint of Harlequin (UK) Limited.
Harlequin (UK) Limited, Eton House, 18-24 Paradise Road,
Richmond, Surrey TW9 1SR

© Leah Ashton 2013

ISBN: 978 0 263 23442 8

:wable
ainable
the

Also by Leah Ashton

Secrets and Speed Dating
A Girl Less Ordinary

**Did you know these are also available as eBooks?
Visit www.millsandboon.co.uk**

For Annie—
who has always been way cooler than her big sister
and then went and worked in film, just to rub it in.
Thank you for your endless help and patience as
I researched this book. Any mistakes are mine.
You're awesome, Annie.

CHAPTER ONE

RUBY BELL ESTIMATED her phone rang approximately half a second before her brisk walk was rudely interrupted by an unfortunately located tuft of grass.

More fortunately, she'd had the presence of mind to hold onto said phone during her less than graceful swan-dive onto the dusty paddock floor. A paddock that had once housed a significant number of sheep, but more recently had become the temporary home of a ninety-strong film crew. Thankfully this particular patch of paddock showed no evidence of sheep occupation.

But, at such close range, Ruby had also learnt that the paddock floor was: a) lumpy and b) hard.

'Paul,' Ruby said, wincing slightly as she lifted the phone to her ear. Still lying flat on her belly in the dirt, she shifted her weight in an unsuccessful attempt to avoid the patches of grass that prickled through the thin fabric of her T-shirt and the seeping warmth that had once been her half-drunk cardboard cup of coffee. Just slightly winded, Ruby's voice was a little breathy, but otherwise she sounded about as efficient as always. Good. She'd built a successful career as a production co-ordinator that took her across the globe—regularly—by being sensible, unflappable, no-nonsense Ruby. Tripping over her own feet couldn't even begin to rattle her.

'I need you back at the office,' Paul said, even more flustered than usual. 'There's been a development.'

And that was it—he'd already hung up. Ruby knew it was

impossible to interpret her producer's urgent tone—it was quite possible the sky *was* falling, but about the same odds that one of the runners had simply screwed up his espresso again. Either way, Ruby needed to get her butt into gear.

'You okay, Rubes?'

Ruby glanced up at the worried voice, squinting a little against the early afternoon sun. But, even mostly in shadow— or maybe because of it—the very broad and very solid frame of Bruno, the key grip, was unmistakeable. Beside him stood a couple of the younger grips, looking about as awkward as they always did when they weren't busily carting heavy objects around—plus about half the hair and make-up department. Which made sense, given she'd managed to come crashing to the ground right outside their trailers.

'Of course,' she said, pressing her outflung hands into the soil and levering herself up onto her knees. She waved away Bruno's helpful hand as she plucked at her T-shirt, pulling the coffee-soaked fabric away from her chest. The parts of her not damp and clinging were decorated with a mix of grass stains and a remarkable number of dirt smudges.

Awesome.

But she didn't have time to worry about the state of her outfit just now. Or her hair—running her fingers through her short blonde pixie-cut confirmed only that it was somehow dusty, too.

A moment later she was back on her feet and her day carried on exactly as before—grass stains and the uncomfortable sensation she was covered in a head-to-toe sticky coating of dirt notwithstanding.

'Ruby!' A yell from somewhere to her left. 'Weather tomorrow?'

'Fine. No chance of rain,' she called out, not even slowing her pace. Paul, as always, would've preferred if she'd gained the power of teleportation. In its absence, she just needed to walk even faster than normal.

The cottage that temporarily housed the film's production office was only a few minutes away—tucked to the left beyond the final cluster of shiny black or white trailers and the slightly askew tent city that was catering.

She kept her focus on her path—already well worn into the grass in the two days since they'd set up camp—mentally crossing her fingers for nothing more serious than a coffee-related emergency. So far she'd already dealt with an unexpected script change, a sudden decision to relocate a scene, and an entitled young actress who'd gone temporarily AWOL. And it was only day one of filming.

'Got a minute?' asked Sarah, a slight redhead in charge of the extensive list of extras required for *The Land*—an 'epic historical romance played out in the heart of the outback'—from the top stair of a shiny black trailer.

'No,' Ruby said, but slowed anyway. 'Paul,' she said, as way of explanation.

'Ah,' Sarah replied, then skipped down from the trailer to fall into step with Ruby as she passed. 'Just a quick one. I've got a call from a concerned parent. They're worried about how we're going to get Samuel to cry in tomorrow's scene.'

By the time she'd reached the last of the row of trailers a minute later, Sarah was on her way with a solution, and Ruby had fielded another phone call on her mobile. Arizona Smith's assistant wanted to know if there were Ashtanga Yoga classes in Lucyville, the small north-west New South Wales country town in which they were filming.

Given the remote town's population was just under two thousand people, Ruby considered this unlikely—but still, with a silent sigh, promised to get back to their female lead's assistant asap.

Ruby broke into a jog as she turned the corner, her gaze trained downward—she wasn't about to hit the dirt again today—and her brain chock-full of potential 'developments' and their hypothetical impact on her already tight schedule.

Consequently, the first she knew of the very large man walking around the corner in the opposite direction was when she slammed straight into him.

'Ooomph!' The slightly strangled sound burst from her throat at the impact of her body hitting solid muscle. She barely registered her hands sliding up sun-warmed arms to grip T-shirt clad shoulders for balance, or the way her legs tangled with his.

What she *did* notice, however, were his hands, strong and firm at her waist, the fingers of one hand hot against bare skin where her T-shirt had ridden an inch or two upwards.

And the scent of his skin, even through the thin layer of cotton, where her face was pressed hard against his chest.

Fresh, clean. *Delicious.*

Oh, my.

'Hey,' he said, his voice deep and a little rough beside her ear. 'You okay?'

Slowly, slowly, embarrassment began to trickle through her body.

No, not embarrassment—the realisation that she *should* be embarrassed, that she *should* be extricating herself from this… *clinch*…as soon as possible.

'Mmm-hmm', she said indistinctly, and didn't move at all.

His fingers flexed slightly, and she registered that now she was moving. Then her back pressed against the cool metal of the shaded wall of a trailer, and she was sliding downwards. He'd been holding her—her feet dangling. Somehow she'd had no idea of this fact until her ballet flats were again responsible for holding her upright.

Had anyone ever held her so effortlessly?

She was medium height, far from tiny—and yet this man had been holding her in his arms as if she weighed as much as the average lollypop-thin Hollywood lead actress.

Nice.

Again his hands squeezed at her waist.

'Hey,' he repeated. 'You're worrying me here. Are you hurt?'

She blinked and finally lifted her head from his chest. She tried to look at him, to figure out who he was—but his face was mostly in shadow, the sunlight a white glare behind him.

But something about the angle of his jaw was familiar.

Who was he? He was fit, but he wasn't one of the grips. Some of the guys in Props were pretty tall, but Ruby honestly couldn't imagine enjoying being held in the arms of any of them. Which she was, undeniably, doing right now. Enjoying this.

She shook her head, trying to focus. 'Just a bit dazed, I think,' she managed. Belatedly, she acknowledged that was true. With every second, the fog was dissipating. But it was a gradual transition.

Right now, she found herself perfectly happy where she was. Standing right where she was.

'Are *you* okay?' she asked.

She could barely make out the slightest curve to his lips, but it was there. 'I'll survive.'

His grip on her softened a little as he seemed to realise she wasn't in any imminent danger. But he didn't let her go. Her hands still rested on his shoulders, but removing them wasn't even a consideration.

A cloud shifted or something, and the shadows lightened. Now she could make out the square line of his jaw, covered liberally in stubble; the sculpted straightness of his nose, and the almost horizontal slashes of his eyebrows. But even this close—close enough that the action of breathing almost brought her chest up against his—she couldn't quite make out the colour of his gaze.

A gaze that she knew was trained on her, exploring her face—her eyes, her lips…

Ruby closed her eyes tight shut, trying to assemble her thoughts. Trying to assemble herself, actually.

The fog had cleared. Reality was re-entering—*her* reality. Straightforward, straight-talking Ruby Bell. Who was *not* taken to romantic notions or embracing total strangers.

He wasn't crew. He must be an extra, some random guy minding his own business before she'd literally thrown herself into his arms.

Inwardly, she cringed. Too late, mortification hit. Hard.

Rational, no-nonsense words were right on the tip of her tongue as she opened her eyes.

But instead of speaking, she sucked in a sharp breath.

He'd moved closer. So, *so* close.

The man didn't look worried now. He looked almost…predatory. In a very, very good way.

She swallowed. Once, twice.

He smiled.

Beneath traitorous fingers that had crept along his shoulders to his nape, his overlong hair was coarse beneath her fingertips.

'You,' he said, his breath fanning against her cheek, 'are quite the welcoming party.'

Ruby felt overwhelmed by him. His size, his devastating looks, his nearness. She barely made out what he'd said. 'Pardon?'

He didn't repeat himself, he just watched her, his gaze locked onto hers.

Whatever she'd been going to say—the words had evaporated.

All she seemed capable of was staring at him. Into those eyes, those amazing, piercing…*familiar* blue eyes.

Finally it clicked into place.

'Has anyone ever told you, you look *just* like Devlin Cooper?' she said. Babbled, maybe. *God.* She didn't know what was going on.

One of his hands had released her waist, and he ran a finger down her cheek and along her jaw. She shivered.

'A couple of times,' he said, the words as dry as the grass they stood upon.

No, not quite like the famous Devlin Cooper. This man had dark circles beneath his eyes, and his darkest blond hair was far too long. He was too tall, surely, as well—she'd met enough leading men to know the average Hollywood star was far shorter than they looked on screen. And, she acknowledged, there was a sparseness to his width—he was muscled, but he didn't have the bulk of the movie star. He looked like Devlin Cooper might look if turned into one of those method actors who lost bucket-loads of weight for a role. Not that Ruby could imagine that ever happening—Devlin Cooper was more generic-action-blockbuster-star than the Oscar-worthy-art-house type.

But as the man's fingers tipped her chin upwards any thought of Devlin Cooper was obliterated. Once again it was just her, and this man, and this amazing, crazy tension that crackled between them. She'd never felt anything like it.

She was sure she'd never wanted anything more than to discover what was going to happen next.

He leant forward, closing the gap between their lips until it was almost non-existent…

Something—a voice nearby maybe—made Ruby jump, and the sound of her shoulders bouncing against the trailer was loud in the silence. A silence she was suddenly terribly aware of.

That rapidly forgotten wave of mortification crashed back over her, this time impossible to ignore. With it, other—less pleasant—sensations than his touch shoved their way to the fore. The fact she was covered in dirt and drying coffee. The fact her whole body suddenly appeared capable of a head to toe, hot, appalled blush.

She was still hanging off the man like a monkey, and she snatched her hands away from his neck.

'Hey. You're not going to catch anything,' he said, a lightness in his tone as he watched her unconsciously wipe her hands almost desperately against her thighs.

She stilled the movement and met his gaze. His eyes had an unreadable glint to them, and for the first time she noticed their thin spidery lines of bloodshot red.

'Who are you?' she asked in a sharp whisper.

His lips curled again, but he didn't say a word. He just watched her, steadily, calmly.

He was infuriating.

She ducked to her left, and the hand that had remained on her waist fell away. Ridiculously, she missed the warmth and weight of his touch immediately, and so she shook her head, desperate to refocus.

She put a few steps between them, taking deep, what-the-heck-just-happened breaths as she glanced to her left and right.

They were alone. No one else stood in this path amongst the trailer metropolis.

No one had seen them.

Relief swamped her. *What on earth had she been thinking?*

But then approaching footsteps made her freeze, as if whoever walked around the corner would immediately know what had just happened.

Of course, it was Paul.

'Ruby!' her producer exclaimed loudly. 'There you are.'

'Ruby,' the man repeated, slowly and softly, behind her. 'Nice name.'

She shot him a glare. Couldn't he just *disappear?* Her mind raced as she tried to determine exactly how long it had been since she'd barrelled into the man. Surely not more than a few minutes?

It wasn't like Paul to come looking for her. Fume alone in his office if she were late, yes—but come find her? Definitely not.

It *must* be a real emergency.

'I'm sorry,' Ruby managed, finally, and meant it. But how to explain? She ran a hand through her hair; the movement dislodged a few forgotten blades of grass. 'I fell over,' she said, more confidently, then nodded in the man's direction. 'He was just helping me up.'

She smoothed her hands down her shirt and its collection of dust, coffee and grass stains for further effect.

There. All sorted, the perfect explanation for why she wasn't in Paul's office five minutes ago.

Out of the corner of her eye, the man grinned. He'd propped himself up against the trailer, ankles crossed—as casual as you like. A normal person would surely size up the situation, realise something was up and—she didn't know—do anything *but* act as if all he were missing were a box of popcorn and a choc-top.

'Thanks for your help,' she said, vaguely in his direction. For the first time she noticed the matching coffee-coloured marks all over the man's grey T-shirt, but she couldn't make herself apologise. He was just too frustratingly calm and oblivious. He could keep his smug smile and newly stained T-shirt.

She walked up to Paul, assuming they'd now go back to his office. 'So, what do you need me to do?'

Paul blinked, his gaze flicking over her shoulder to the man that *still* stood so nonchalantly behind her.

'You left in a hurry,' he said—not to Ruby, but to the man.

Ruby turned on her heel, looking from Paul to the man and back again—completely confused.

The man shrugged. 'I had things to do.'

Paul's eyes narrowed and his lips thinned, as if he was on the verge of one of his explosions.

But then—instead—he cleared his throat, and turned to Ruby. A horrible sense of foreboding settled in her stomach.

'So you've met our new leading man.'

She spoke without thinking. 'Who?'

There was a barely muffled laugh behind her.

The man. His knowing smile. The charisma that oozed from every pore.

Finally, *finally,* she connected the dots.

This was Paul's latest drama. *This* was why she'd been rushing back to the office.

They had a new leading man.

She'd just met him.

She'd just covered him in dirt and coffee.

Worst of all—she'd just nearly *kissed* him.

And he didn't just have a passing resemblance to Devlin Cooper. A passing resemblance to a man who commanded double-digit multimillion-dollar salaries and provided continuous tabloid fodder to the world's magazines and salacious television entertainment reports. A man who'd long ago left Australia and now was mentioned in the same breath as Brad, and George, and Leo…

'You can call me Dev,' he said, his voice deep and oh-so intimate.

Oh.

My.

God.

Dev Cooper smiled as the slender blonde raked her fingers desperately through her short-cropped hair.

Ruby.

It suited her. She was striking: with big, velvety brown eyes
beneath dark blonde brows, sharp-edged cheekbones and a lush
mouth. Maybe her elegant nose was a little too long, and her
chin a little too stubborn—if she were a model his agent had
picked out for him to be photographed with at some premiere
or opening or whatever.

But, thankfully, she wasn't. It would seem she was a member
of the crew of this film he was stuck working on for the next six
weeks. And—if the way she'd been looking at him a few minutes earlier was anything to go by—she was going to make the
next few days, maybe longer, a heck of a lot more interesting.

Ruby crossed her arms as she spoke to the producer—Phil?
No, *Paul.* The man who'd owed his agent Veronica a favour.
A really *big* favour, it turned out, given his agent had bundled
him onto the plane to Sydney *before* she'd sorted out the pesky
little detail of whether or not he had the role.

Dev guessed, knowing Veronica, that Paul had discovered
he was replacing his leading man just before Dev had turned
up in his shiny black hire car. Chauffeur driven, of course—his
agent was taking no chances this time.

He shifted his weight a little, easing the pressure on his left
leg, which throbbed steadily. Had it really only been a week?

The pancake-flat countryside where he now stood couldn't
be further away from his driveway in Beverly Hills—the site of
'the last straw' as his agent had put it. Even Dev had to admit
that forgetting to put his car into reverse wasn't his best moment.
Ditto to driving into his living room, and writing off his Jag.

On the plus side, he hadn't been injured, beyond some temporary muscle damage, and, thanks to the fortress-style wall that surrounded his house, no one beyond his agent and long-suffering housekeeper even knew it had happened.

And, despite what Veronica believed, he hadn't been drunk.

Exhausted after not sleeping for four nights—yes. But driving, or attempting to drive, drunk? No, he hadn't slid that low. *Yet?*

Dev scrubbed at his eyes, uninterested in pursuing the direction his thoughts had taken him. Instead, he refocused on Ruby and Paul, who had stopped talking and were now looking at him.

Ruby's gaze was direct, despite the hint of colour at her cheeks. She was embarrassed, no doubt. But she was brazening it out.

He liked that.

'I'm Ruby Bell,' she said, 'Production Co-ordinator for *The Land.*'

Her arm moved slightly, as though she was going to shake his hand before thinking better of it.

A shame. He was impatient to touch her again.

Maybe she saw some of what he was thinking, as her eyes narrowed. But her tone revealed nothing. 'Paul will give me your details, and I'll send through tomorrow's call sheet once I've spoken to the assistant director.'

He nodded.

Then Paul started talking, putting lots of emphasis on *tight timelines* and *stop dates* and *getting up to speed as quickly as possible*—all things he'd said in their abruptly truncated meeting earlier.

Lord, anyone would think he made a habit of missing his call...

He smiled tightly at his private joke, eliciting a glare from Paul.

Dev tensed. This film might have a decent budget for an Australian production, but it was no Hollywood blockbuster. He was replacing a *soapie star* as the lead, for heaven's sake.

No way was he going to take a thinly veiled lecture from some nobody producer.

'I get it,' he said, cutting him off mid-stream, the action not dissimilar to what had happened in Paul's office when he'd had enough of his blustering. 'I'll see you both,' he said, pausing to catch Ruby's gaze, 'tomorrow.'

And with that, he was off.

Six weeks of filming. Six weeks to placate his agent.

Six weeks working in a town out beyond the middle of nowhere. Where—he knew his agent hoped—even Dev Cooper couldn't get into any trouble.

A heated memory of chocolate eyes that sparkled and urgent fingers threaded through his hair made him smile.

Well, he hadn't made any promises.

CHAPTER TWO

IT TOOK ALL of Ruby's strength to follow Paul up the small flight of brick steps to the production office. She literally had to remind herself to place one foot in front of the other, as her body really, *really* wanted to carry her in the opposite direction. *Away* from the scene of unquestionably one of the most humiliating moments of her career. Her life, even.

How could she not have recognised him?

Only the possibility that any attempted escape could lead her back to Devlin Cooper stopped her. Oh—and the fact she kind of loved her career.

As they walked down the narrow hallway of the dilapidated cottage/temporary production office, Paul explained in twenty-five words or less that Mr Cooper was replacing Todd, effective immediately. That was it—no further explanation.

By now they'd made it to Paul's makeshift kitchen-cum-office at the rear of the cottage. Inside stood Sal, the line producer, and Andy, the production manager. They both wore matching, serious expressions.

It was enough to force Ruby to pull herself together. She needed to focus on the job at hand—i.e. coordinating this movie with a completely new star.

'I have to ask,' asked Andy, his fingers hooked in the belt loops of his jeans. 'How the hell did you get Devlin Cooper to take this role?'

Ruby thought Paul might have rolled his eyes, but couldn't be sure. 'Let's just say that the opportunity arose. So I took it.'

Despite the catastrophic impact on their immovable filming schedule, Ruby could hardly blame him. With Devlin's star power, *The Land* would reach a whole new audience. Why Devlin *took* the role was another question entirely—did he want to spend time back in Australia? Did he feel a need to give back to the Australian film industry? A chance to take on a role well outside his vanilla action-hero stereotype?

It didn't really matter.

Filming had started, and Dev's character Seth was in nearly every scene. Tomorrow's call sheet had Todd's name all over it—the guy who Dev had replaced. Unquestionably, they'd lost tomorrow. Which was not good, as Arizona had to be at Pinewood Studios in London for her next film in just six weeks and one day's time. They didn't have *any* time up their sleeves.

'Does Dev know the script?'

Paul just looked at her. *What do you think?*

Okay. So they'd lost more than just tomorrow. Dev would need to rehearse. Ruby's mind scrambled about trying to figure out how the first assistant director could possibly rearrange the filming schedule that she'd so painstakingly put together… and she'd need to organise to get Dev's costumes sorted. And his hair cut. And…

'Should I sort out a medical appointment?' she asked. A doctor's report for each actor was required for the film's insurance—everything from a propensity for cold sores through to a rampant base-jumping hobby had an impact on how much it cost.

'No,' Paul said, very quickly.

Ruby tilted her head, studying him. But before she could ask the obvious question, Paul explained. 'He saw a doctor in Sydney when he landed. It's all sorted.'

Okay. She supposed that made sense.

'Accommodation?'

God knew where she'd put him. The cast and crew had already overrun every bed and breakfast plus the local—rather cosy—motel.

'He's taking over Todd's place.'

Ouch. Poor Todd. He must be devastated—this role was widely considered his big break. He was being touted as the *next big thing.*

Only to be trumped by the current big thing.

She felt for him, but, unfortunately, the brutality of this industry never failed to surprise her.

This was not a career for the faint-hearted, or anyone who needed the reassurance of a job associated with words like *stable,* or *reliable.*

Fortunately, that was exactly why Ruby loved it.

Ten minutes later, the four of them had a plan of sorts for the next few days, and she was closing Paul's office door behind her as Sal and Andy rushed back to their desks.

For a moment she stood, alone, in the cottage's narrow old hallway. Noise spilled from the two rooms that flanked it: music, clattering keyboards, multiple conversations and the occasional burst of laughter. A familiar hum peppered with familiar voices.

To her left was Sal and Andy's office. Ruby didn't need to glance through their open doorway to know they'd already be busily working away on the trestle-tables that served as their temporary desks. The office would also be perfectly organised— notepads and pens all lined up, that kind of thing—because it always was. They were in charge of the film's budget—so such meticulous organisation was definitely a plus.

In theory, given her own role, she should be just as meticulous.

Instead, to her right was the room that, amongst other things, housed her own trestle-table desk, many huge prone-to-collapsing mountains of paper and only the vaguest sense of order. Or so it appeared, anyway. She had to be ruthlessly organised— but she didn't need to be tidy to be effective.

The room was also the home of the three members of the production crew who reported to her—Cath, Rohan and Selena. Unsurprisingly, it was this room where the majority of noise was coming from, as this was the happening part of the production office where all day every day they managed actors and scripts and agents and vendors and anything or anyone else needed to keep the film going. It was crazy, demanding, noisy work—and with a deep breath, she walked straight into it.

As expected, three heads popped up as she stepped through the door.

'I guess you all heard the news?'

As one, they nodded.

'Was kind of awesome when he walked out on Paul,' said Rohan, leaning back in his chair. 'Paul came in here and ranted for a bit before charging out the door in pursuit. Guess he couldn't find him.'

Ruby didn't bother to correct him.

Instead, she spent a few minutes further explaining the situation, and assigning them all additional tasks. No one complained—quite the opposite, actually. No one saw the unexpected addition of a major star to *The Land* as anything but a very good thing. It meant they were all instantly working on a film far bigger than they'd signed up for. It was a fantastic opportunity.

She needed to remember that.

Ruby settled herself calmly into her chair, dropping her phone onto her desk—fortunately no worse for wear after hitting the dirt for the second time today. She tapped the mouse track pad on her laptop, and it instantly came to life, displaying the twenty-odd new emails that had arrived since she'd last had a chance to check her phone. Not too bad given it seemed like a lifetime since she'd been busily redistributing those last-minute script revisions to the actors.

She had a million and one things to do, and she really needed to get straight back to it. Instead, her attention skidded about the room—away from her glowing laptop screen and out of the window. There wasn't much of a view—just bare, flat countryside all the way to the ridge of mountains—but she wasn't really looking at it. Instead, her brain was still desperately trying to process the events of the past half-hour.

It didn't seem possible that she'd so recently been wrapped around one of the sexiest men in the world.

While covered in dirt.

And had had absolutely no idea.

Inwardly, she cringed for about the thousandth time.

Work. She reminded herself. She just needed to focus on work. Who cared if she'd accidentally flung herself into Devlin Cooper's arms? It was an accident, and it would never happen again—after all, she wasn't exactly anywhere near Dev Cooper's percentile on the drop-dead-gorgeousness spectrum. And he'd hardly had the opportunity to be attracted to her sparkling personality.

Despite everything, that thought made her smile.

No. This wasn't funny. This was serious. What if someone had seen them?

She stood up, as sitting still had become impossible. On the window sill sat the antenna of their oversized wireless Internet router, and she fiddled with it, just so it looked as if she were doing something constructive. On a location this remote, they'd had to bring their own broadband. And their own electricity, actually—provided by a large truck that's sole purpose was to power Unit Base, the name of this collection of trucks and people that were the beating heart of any feature film.

Her job was everything to her, and a spotless professional reputation was non-negotiable. She didn't get each job by circling ads in the paper, or subscribing to some online jobs database. In film, it was *all* about word of mouth.

And getting it on with an actor on set… Yeah. Not a good look.

On the plus side, Dev would have forgotten all about the slightly mussed-up, damp and dusty woman who'd gang-tackled him by now.

Now she just needed to forget about how he'd made her feel.

I think some time away would do you good. Help you…move on.
Well. Dev guessed this place was exactly what Veronica had

been hoping for. A painstakingly restored century-old cottage, complete with tasteful rear extension, was where he'd be calling home for the immediate future. It offered uninterrupted views to the surrounding mountains and everything!

It was also a kilometre or so out of town, had no immediate neighbours, and, thanks to his agent, a live-in minder.

Security. Officially.

Right.

He needed a drink. He'd walked off a trans-Pacific flight less than eight hours ago. Even travelling first class couldn't make a flight from LA to Sydney pleasant. Add a four-hour road trip with Graeme-the-security-guy and was it surprising he'd had a short fuse today?

Please play nice with Paul.

This in his latest email from his agent.

He shouldn't have been surprised that the producer had already started updating Veronica on his behaviour. He'd even learnt exactly what she'd held over the prickly producer—knowledge of an on-set indiscretion with an aspiring actress ten years previously.

What a cliché.

And how like his agent to file that little titbit away for future use.

Good for her. Although he didn't let himself consider how exactly he'd got to this point—to where landing roles depended on tactics and calling in favours.

Dev had dragged an overstuffed armchair onto the rear decking. On his lap was the script for *The Land,* not that he could read it now the sun had long set.

Beside him, on one of the chairs from the wooden outdoor setting he'd decided looked too uncomfortable, was his dinner. Cold, barely touched salmon with fancy-looking vegetables. God knew where Veronica had sourced his fridge and freezer full of food from—he'd long ago got used to her magic touch.

Although the lack of alcohol hadn't gone unnoticed. *Subtle, Veronica.*

But she was wrong. Booze wasn't his problem.

He'd have to send good old Graeme down to the local bottle shop tomorrow or something.

But for now, he needed a drink.

Leaving the script on the chair, he walked through the house, and then straight out of the front door. Graeme was staying in a separate, smaller worker's cottage closer to the road, but Dev didn't bother to stop and let him know where he was going.

He'd been micro-managed quite enough. He could damn well walk into town and get a drink without having to ask anyone's approval.

So he did.

Walking felt good. For once he wasn't on the lookout for the paparazzi, as, for now, no one knew he was here. His unexpected arrival in Australia would have been noticed, of course, and it wouldn't take long before the photographers descended. But they hadn't, not just yet.

He had no idea what time it was, just that it was dark. Really dark—there were certainly no streetlights, and the moon was little more than a sliver.

His boots were loud on the bitumen, loud enough to disturb a group of sheep that scattered abruptly behind their barbed-wire fence. Further from the road nestled the occasional house, their windows glowing squares of bright amid the darkness.

Soon he'd hit the main street, a short stretch of shops, a petrol station, a library. He hadn't paid much attention when he'd arrived—a mix of jet lag and general lack of interest—but now he took the time to look, slowing his walk down to something approaching an amble.

Most of the town was silent—blinds were drawn, shops were certainly closed this late. But the one obvious exception was the pub, which, like much of the town, was old and stately—perched two storeys high on a corner, complete with a wide wooden balcony overlooking the street. Tonight the balcony was empty, but noise and music spilled from the open double doors. He quickened his pace, suddenly over all this peace and quiet.

It was packed. Completely—people were crammed at the bar, around the scattered tall tables and also the lower coffee tables with their surrounding couches and ottomans. It was the cast and crew, obviously, who'd taken the pub over. He'd seen for himself that Lucyville didn't exactly have a happening restaurant strip. This was the only place to drink—and eat—so here they all were.

The pub didn't go quiet or anything at his arrival, but he noticed that he'd been noticed.

It was a sensation that had once been a novelty, had later annoyed him to the verge of anger—and now that he just accepted. He could hardly complain…he was living his dream and all that.

Right.

He found a narrow gap at the bar, resting an arm on the polished surface. The local bartender caught his eye and did a double take, but played it cool. In his experience, most people did, with the occasional crazy person the exception rather than the rule. The paparazzi were far more an issue than Joe Public—no question.

He ordered his drink, although he wasn't quick to raise the glass to his lips once it was placed in front of him. Maybe it wasn't the drink he'd needed, but the walk, the bite of the crisp night air in his lungs?

Mentally he shook his head. Veronica would love that, be all smug and sure she was right to send him to Australia—while Dev wasn't so certain.

What was that saying? Same crap—different bucket.

His lips tightened into a humourless smile.

He turned, propping his weight against the bar. As he took a sip of his beer he surveyed the large room. It was a surprisingly eclectic place, with funky modern furniture managing to blend with the polished ancient floorboards and what—he was pretty sure—was the original bar. Not quite the backwater pub he'd been imagining.

The lighting was soft and the atmosphere relaxed, with the dress code more jeans than cocktail.

One particular pair of jeans caught his eye. Dark blue denim, moulded over elegantly crossed legs—right in the corner of the pub, the one farthest from him.

Yet his attention had still been drawn to her, to Ruby.

Only when he saw her did he realise he'd been looking for her—searching her out in the crowd.

He watched her as she talked to her friends, wine glass in hand. To all appearances she was focused completely on the conversation taking place around her. She was quick to smile, and quick to interject and trigger a laugh from others. But despite all that, there was the slightest hint of tension to her body.

She knew he was watching her.

Beside her, another woman leant over and whispered in her ear, throwing glances in his direction as she did.

Ruby shook her head emphatically—and Dev was no lip-reader, but he'd put money on the fact she'd just said: *No, he's not.*

Accordingly, he straightened, pushing himself away from the bar.

He liked nothing more than to prove someone wrong.

'He's coming over!'

Every single cell in Ruby's body—already tingling at what she'd told herself was Dev's imagined attention—careened up to high alert.

'It's no big deal. We met before.' She shrugged deliberately. 'Maybe he doesn't know anyone else yet.'

'*When* did you meet him?' Selena asked, wide-eyed. 'And how am I not aware of this?'

Ruby's words were carefully cool. 'When I was walking back to the office. We barely said two words.'

That, at least, was completely true.

Her friend had lost interest, anyway, her eyes trained on Dev's tall frame as he approached.

'Mind if I join you?'

Dev's voice was as gorgeously deep and perfect as in every

one of his movies. Not for the first time, Ruby questioned her intelligence—how on *earth* had she not recognised him?

With a deep breath, she lifted her gaze to meet his. He stood on the other side of the table before them: Ruby, Selena and a couple of girls from the art department. They'd been having an after-dinner drink, all comfy on one big plush purple L-shaped couch—now the other three were alternating between carefully feigned disinterest and slack-jawed adoration. Unheard of for professionals in the film industry who dealt with stars every day.

But, she supposed, this *was* Devlin Cooper.

Everyone else appeared struck dumb and incapable of answering his question—but Dev was looking at her, anyway.

To say *yes, she did mind,* was tempting—but more trouble than it was worth. So, reluctantly, she shook her head. 'Not at all.'

Dev stepped past the table and sat next to Ruby.

With great effort, she resisted the temptation to scoot away. Unlike the three other women at the table, she was *not* going to treat Dev any differently from anyone else on the cast and crew.

No adoring gaze. No swooning.

So, although he was close—and the couch definitely no longer felt *big*—she didn't move. Didn't betray one iota of the unexpected heat that had flooded her body.

'You shouldn't be embarrassed,' he said, low enough that only she could hear.

'Why would you think I am?'

Casually, she brought her glass to her lips.

Did he notice the slightest trembling of her fingers?

She risked a glance out of the corner of her eye.

He watched her with a familiar expression. Confident. Knowing.

Arrogant.

She sighed. 'Fine. I *was* embarrassed. Let me think: running into one of the world's most famous men, while covered in dirt and looking like crap—*and* then not even recognising said star...' Ruby tilted her head, as if considering her words.

'Yes, I think that pretty much sums it up. I reckon a good nine out of ten on my embarrassment scale.'

He didn't even blink. If anything he looked amused.

A different type of tension stiffened her body. Yes, her stupid, apparently one-track body was all a-flutter with Mr Hot Movie Star so near. But now she could add affronted frustration into the mix.

She didn't know what she wanted—an apology? Sympathy? A *yeah, I can see how that might've sucked for you,* even?

'But you only gave it a nine,' he said, placing his beer on one of the discarded coasters on the table.

'A what?' she asked, confused.

'On your *embarrassment scale,*' he said. 'Only a nine…' He looked contemplative for a moment, then leant closer, close enough that it was impossible for her to look anywhere but straight into his eyes. 'So I was wondering—what would've made it a ten?'

Immediately, and most definitely without her volition, her gaze dropped from his piercing blue eyes to his lips.

Lips that immediately quirked into a grin the second she realised what she'd done. What she'd just revealed.

He leant even closer again. The touch of his breath on the sensitive skin beneath her ear made her shiver.

Logically she knew she should pull away, that she should laugh loudly, or say something—*do something*—to stop this way too intimate moment. A moment she knew was being watched—and if people were watching, then people would gossip.

And there were few things Ruby hated more than gossip: being the subject of *or* the proliferation of it.

For she had far too much experience in the former. Enough to last a lifetime.

'You know,' he said, his words somehow vibrating through her body—her stupidly frozen body, 'I don't think anyone's ever been embarrassed when I've kissed them. In fact, I'm quite sure I've never received a complaint.'

Oh, she was so sure he hadn't…

'I was working,' she said, each word stiff and awkward.

So he had been going to kiss her—and she realised it was no surprise. Some part of her had known, had known there was no other way to interpret those few minutes, even though her rational self had had so much difficulty believing it.

But knowing she hadn't imagined it and *wanting* it to have happened were entirely different things.

'I kiss people all the time at work,' he replied, with a spark of humour in his eyes that was new, and unexpected.

Ruby found herself forcing back a grin, surprised at the shift in atmosphere. 'It's a bit different when you're following a script.'

'Ah,' he said, his lips quirking up. 'Not always.'

Now she laughed out loud, shaking her head. 'I bet.'

Their laughter should've diluted the tension, but if anything the air between them thickened.

With great effort, Ruby turned away slightly, taking a long, long sip of her wine—not that she tasted a thing. Her brain whirred at a million miles an hour—or maybe it wasn't whirring at all, considering all it seemed to be able to do was wonder how Dev's lips would feel against hers...

No.

'Well,' she said, finally, her gaze swinging back to meet his. Firmly. 'Script or otherwise, I don't kiss anyone at work.' She paused, then added in a tone that was perfectly matter-of-fact and perfectly polite, 'It's late. I need to go. It was nice to talk to you when I wasn't covered in dirt. And I'm sorry about your T-shirt.'

Ruby stood up and placed her wine glass on the table with movements she hoped looked casual. She glanced at her friends, who all stared at her wide-eyed.

She'd need to set them all straight tomorrow. Dev Cooper was so not her type it was ridiculous.

She managed some goodbyes, hooked her handbag over her shoulder, and then headed for the door. The entire time she risked barely a glance at Dev, but thankfully he didn't move.

Not that she expected him to follow her. She wasn't an idiot. He could have any woman in this bar. Pretty much any woman in the *world*.

For some reason she'd piqued his interest, but she had no doubt it was fleeting—the novelty of the crazy dusty coffee lady or something.

Outside, the early October evening was cool, and so Ruby hugged herself, rubbing her goose-pimpling arms. She was staying at the town motel, not even a hundred-metre walk down the main street.

Only a few steps in that direction, she heard someone else leave the bar behind her, their boots loud on the wooden steps.

It was difficult, but as it turned out not impossible, to keep her eyes pointed forward. It could be anyone.

'Ruby.'

Or it could be Dev.

She should've sighed—and been annoyed or disappointed. But instead her tummy lightened and she realised she was smiling.

Ugh.

She kept on walking.

In moments, following the thud of loping strides on bitumen, he was beside her, keeping pace with her no-nonsense walk. For long seconds, they walked in silence.

Really uncomfortable, charged silence.

'So—' he began.

'This isn't an act, you know,' Ruby interrupted. 'I'm not playing hard to get. I'm not interested.'

He gave a surprised bark of laughter. 'Right.'

Ruby slowed to a stop, her whole body stiff with annoyance. She stood beneath a street lamp that illuminated the gate to the *Lucyville Motel* and its chipped and faded sign.

'You sound so sure,' she said. 'That's incredibly presumptuous.'

'Am I wrong?'

Ruby sighed. 'Does every woman you meet *really* collapse into a pathetic puddle of lust at your feet?'

'You did,' he pointed out.

Her cheeks went hot, but Ruby hoped her blush was hidden in the shadows.

'I was light-headed. Confused. Definitely not myself.' She paused for emphasis. 'Trust me. You're wasting your time. *I'm not interested.*'

A little, nagging voice at the back of her mind kept trying to distract her: *Oh, my God, it's Devlin Cooper! The movie star!*

Maybe that was why she didn't turn and walk away immediately.

'You're serious?'

His genuine confusion was rather endearing. Unbelievably conceited, but endearing.

'Uh-huh,' she said, nodding. 'Is that so hard to believe?'

She knew he was about to say *yes,* when he seemed to realise what he was about to say. Instead, his grin, revealed by the streetlight, was bemused.

He shifted his weight to one leg, and crossed his arms. He still wore the same sexy ancient-looking jeans from before, but he'd traded his ruined T-shirt for its twin in navy blue. The action of crossing his arms only further defined the muscles of his forearms and biceps.

It also defined the unexpectedly sharp angles of his elbows and the lack of flesh beyond his lean musculature.

She knew she was not the only person to notice. The film set's grapevine was, as always, efficient, creating all sorts of theories for his unexpected weight loss.

Did you hear? His girlfriend left him—you know? That model.

I heard it's drugs. Ice. He's been photographed at every club in Hollywood.

He's sick. I know! That's why he's come back to Australia. To spend time with his family.

Not that Ruby believed a word of it. Gossip, in her experi-

ence, was about as accurate and true to life as the typical air-
brushed movie poster.

What happened to you?

But of course the question remained unsaid. It was none of
her business.

Dev studied Ruby in the limited moonlight. His gaze traced the
angles of her cheekbones, the straightness of her nose and the
firm set of her determined mouth.

Lord, she was...pretty?

Yes. Hot?

Yes.

But that, in itself, wasn't *it*...

And different. Very, very, different.

That was why he was standing out in the deserted, frankly
cold, street. That was why he'd done something he couldn't remember doing in a very long time: he'd chased after a woman.

It was an unexpected novelty.

He liked it.

For the first time in months something—*someone*—had
caught his interest. Ruby Bell—the cute little production co-
ordinator on a dinky little Aussie film—intrigued him.

'So what is it, exactly, that you find so repulsive about me?'
he asked.

She shrugged, dismissing his question. 'I don't know you
well enough to form an opinion—repulsive or otherwise.'

'But isn't that why you're not interested?' he asked. Not that
he believed her statement to be true. 'Because you think you
know me?'

From his movies, from his interviews, from the rubbish they
published in glossy magazines and newspapers that should know
better. Devlin Cooper the star—the persona. Not the person.

She shook her head. 'This is the longest conversation we've
ever had. How could I possibly know you?'

He blinked. She'd just surprised him—for the second time
tonight. The first time had been walking out of that pub just as

he'd been imagining how good she'd look in that big wrought-iron bed back in his cottage.

'Ah. So, it's not me, it's *you*,' he said, playing with that cliché line. Then, for the first time, the blindingly obvious occurred to him. She wore no ring, but... 'You have a boyfriend?'

'Oh *no*,' she said, her voice higher pitched and definitely firmer than before. 'Absolutely not.' She shook her head for emphasis.

Okay, now he was completely confused. And surprised, yet again.

Ruby wasn't following any script he'd heard before. How many women had he flirted with in his life? Some fawned, but most were clever, witty and/or sarcastic. But, he realised, normally he already sort of knew what was going to be said next—where the conversation, or the evening, was heading. In itself, that was part of the fun. The dance of words before the inevitable.

But this was undeniably fun, too.

'You think *I* want a relationship?' he asked, heavy with irony. 'Scared I'm going to want to settle down, get married...'

She laughed. 'No.'

'So what, exactly, is the problem? From where I stand this all seems pretty perfect. We obviously both like each other...' he held up his hand when she went to disagree '...we're both single *and* we're both stuck in an isolated country town for the next month or so. Is that not a match made in heaven?'

Ruby rolled her eyes. 'Weren't you listening back at the pub? I don't do relationships at work. *Especially* with actors. I'm not interested in becoming known as Dev Cooper's next conquest. *Très* professional, no?'

'I wasn't suggesting we make out on set, you know,' he said dryly. Ruby raised an eyebrow. 'I promise.'

She shook her head. 'Film sets are full of gossip. And my professional reputation is everything to me.' She paused, then repeated her words, almost to herself. '*Everything* to me.'

Commitment to your job—sure, Dev got that. Until very

recently, he'd practically been the poster child for the concept. But—really? Liaisons between crew and actors were not a crime, and far from uncommon. The world would not end.

But apparently, according to Ruby, it would. It was clear in every tense line of her expression.

They stood in silence for a while. Dev wasn't entirely sure what would happen now.

He was out of his element: he'd just been rejected. Inarguably so.

But rather than shrugging, comfortable in the knowledge that he had many other options, he found himself...disappointed.

And reluctant to walk away.

'Anyway,' Ruby said in a different, crisper, tone. 'You have an early call tomorrow morning, and I need to be at the office an hour earlier. So, goodnight.'

With that, she turned on her heel and walked away. Out on the street he watched as she walked down the motel driveway to an apartment on the bottom floor of the two-storey building. Then he waited until she located her key in her oversized handbag, unlocked the door, and disappeared inside.

Then he waited, alone on the street, some more.

It was odd. All he knew about this woman was that she was blonde, and cute, and felt pretty amazing in his arms.

What was the attraction? Why did he care?

How was she different from the many other women who he'd met in the past few, dark, blurry months? Months where no one had stood out. Where *nothing* had stood out.

Where when, a few weeks after Estelle had left, he'd attempt to chat to a woman—but his mind would drift. Where he'd find himself with suddenly no idea what had been said in the preceding conversation.

And didn't care at all.

That was why she was different.

Ruby pushed his buttons. Triggered reactions that had been lying dormant. Attraction. Laughter. Surprise.

So simple.

CHAPTER THREE

A LOUD BANG jolted Dev out of his dream.

He blinked, his eyes attempting to adjust to the darkness.

What time is it?

He lay on his back in the centre of his bed. Naked but for his boxer shorts, the sheets and quilt long ago kicked off and onto the floor.

He remembered feeling restless. As if he needed to get up and go for a run. Or for a drive. Or just *out*. Somewhere. Away.

Where?

It wasn't the first morning he'd asked that question.

Another bang. Even louder than before. Or maybe just now he was more awake?

The thick cloak of sleep was slowly lifting, and his eyes were adjusting.

It wasn't completely dark in here. Light was managing to push through the heavy curtains that he'd checked and double checked were fully closed the night before.

He shivered, and only then did he register it was cold. He had a vague recollection of turning off the heater on the wall. Why? The nights were still cool.

Obviously it had made sense at the time.

Another bang.

The door. Someone was knocking on the door.

What time is it?

He rolled onto his side, reaching across the bed, knocking aside a small cardboard box and a blister pack so he could see the glowing green numbers of the clock on the bedside table. There were none. He didn't remember turning it off, but it didn't surprise him that he had.

He had set that alarm last night, though. And the alarm on his phone. He had an early call today. He'd been going to get up early to read through today's rehearsal scenes.

Bang, bang, bang.

Dev swung his legs over the side of the bed in slow motion, then shoved himself to his feet. Three sluggish steps later, he discovered his mobile phone when he kicked it in the gloom, and it clattered against his closed bedroom door.

By feel he found the light switch on the wall, then rubbed his eyes against the sudden brightness.

His phone located, he picked it up to check the time. He pressed the button to illuminate the screen, but it took a while for his eyes to focus.

How long ago had he taken the sleepers?

He still felt drugged, still shrouded in the sleep that the tablets had finally delivered.

Seven thirty-two a.m. *Why hadn't his alarm gone off?*

Bang, bang, BANG, BANG, BANG!

'Mr Cooper? Are you awake?'

Graeme. Of course.

He twisted the old brass doorknob to his room, then padded up the wide hallway. Morning light streamed through the stained-glass panels of the front door around the over-inflated shape that was Dev's warden.

He took his time, his gaze trained on his phone as he checked that his alarm had been set. It had. So it had gone off.

Presumably he'd then thrown it across the room, given where he'd found it.

It shouldn't surprise him, but that wasn't what he'd meant to do today. Last night he'd felt...different. Today was supposed to be different. Different from the past ninety-seven days.

How specific.

He smiled a humourless smile. Who knew his subconscious kept such meticulous records?

The thing was, today wasn't the first day that was supposed to be different. But then, they never were.

Graeme was still hammering away at the door, but Dev didn't bother to call out, to reassure him that his charge was in fact awake and not passed out in an alcoholic stupor or worse— whatever it was that Veronica was so sure that Dev was doing.

In some ways Dev wished he could apply a label to himself. *Alcoholic. Drug addict.*

But he was neither of those things.

What about his sleepers?

He dismissed the idea instantly. No. They were prescribed, and temporary.

Definitely temporary.

Hollywood wasn't the shiny happy place people imagined. It was full of egos fuelled by intense insecurity. Stars that shone while simultaneously harbouring the intense fear that their light could be extinguished at any moment: at the mercy of their next role, of public opinion, of the whims of studio executives…always others.

So little control. It was no surprise that so many teetered over the edge. Fell into…*something.* It was just the label that changed.

But Dev had no label.

He just had…nothing.

He opened the door while Graeme was mid-knock. The other man started, then took a step back, clearing his throat.

'We need to leave in five minutes, Mr Cooper.'

Dev scratched his belly and nodded. He left the door open as he turned and headed for the bathroom. Four minutes later he was showered and had dragged on a T-shirt, hoodie and jeans. He pulled the front door shut and locked it as Graeme hovered nearby—impatiently.

When he was growing up, his mum had done the same thing—although not as silently. She'd tap her foot as she waited for her youngest and most disorganised son. The other two boys generally already in the family Mercedes, all perfect and con-sistently smug. *Hurry up, Dev! You're making us late!*

And just because he'd been that kind of kid, he'd taken his own sweet time.

This was why he didn't like having drivers. Why he insisted on driving himself to and from set for every single one of his many movies. He was a grown adult with a driver's licence—why the hell did he need a chauffeur? He was far from a child any more; he didn't need to be directed and herded and hur-ried. He was a professional—always on time. Always reliable.

Until now.

Today was not the first time he'd slept through his alarm. Or, of more concern: he'd heard it, switched it off, and delib-erately rolled over and gone back to sleep. More than once the action of even setting his alarm had felt impossible. Weirdly overwhelming.

Other nights sleep had never come. Where his thoughts had echoed so loudly in his skull that even drugs had no impact. And those days he'd watched time tick by, watched his call time slip by, and switched his phone to silent as his agent, or the producer, or even the director would call, and call and call...

That had got him fired from his last film. The contract was pulled on his next after whispers had begun to spread.

So here he was.

And although he hadn't meant to—because of course he never *meant to*—it was happening again.

Without Graeme, he'd still be in bed, time passing. He hated that.

He sat in the back of the black four-wheel drive, staring un-seeing out of the darkly tinted windows. Beside him was an insulated bag that Graeme said contained his breakfast, but he wasn't hungry.

You're not welcome here.

Closer to Unit Base, the bitumen road ended, and the car bounced amongst potholes on the wide gravel track. The irreg-ular movements did nothing to jolt that memory. How long ago

had it been? Ten years? No, longer. Fourteen. He'd been nineteen, home late—really late—after a night out with his mates.

He hadn't been drunk, but alcohol had still buzzed through
his bloodstream.

'Where the hell have you been?'

*His father stood at the very top of the staircase that rose
majestically from the lobby of the Coopers' sprawling Sydney
upper-north-shore residence. His mum had left a lamp on for
him, and the soft light threw shadows onto his dad's pyjamas.*

'Out,' he said. Grunted, really.

'You have an exam tomorrow.'

*Dev shrugged. He'd had no intention of turning up. He
dumped his keys on a sideboard, and began to head past the
stairs to the hallway that led to his bedroom, tossing his reply
over his shoulder. 'I'm not going to be an accountant, Dad.'*

*Patrick Cooper's slippered feet were still heavy as they
thumped down each carpeted step. Dev didn't pause. He'd
heard it all before.*

*He'd gone to uni to please his mum, only. But three semesters
in, and he'd had it. He knew where his life was leading, and it
didn't involve a calculator and a navy-blue suit.*

*His father picked up his pace behind him, but Dev remained
deliberately slow. Unworried. Casual.*

*He was unsurprised to feel the weight of his father's hand
on his shoulder. But when Dev kept walking, the way Patrick wrenched at his shoulder, spinning him around...yes, that
shocked him.*

*His arm came up, his fingers forming into a fist. It was au-
tomatic, the result of the crowd he'd been hanging with, the
occasional push and shove at a pub. He wouldn't have hit his
dad—he knew that. Knew that.*

*But his dad thought he would. He could see it in his eyes, that
belief of what Dev was capable of. Or rather, the lack of belief.*

*Dev saw the fist coming. Maybe he didn't have enough time
to move, maybe he did—either way he stood stock still.*

His father's knuckles connected with his jaw with enough

force to twist his body and push him back into the wall. And for it to hurt. A lot. He tasted blood, felt it coating his teeth.

But he remained standing, half expecting more.

But that wasn't going to happen. Instead, his dad fell to his knees, holding his fist in his other hand.

For long moments, it was perfectly silent. It was as if neither of them could breathe.

Then a clatter on the stairs heralded his mum's arrival. She gasped as she came into view, then ran to Patrick, kneeling beside him and wrapping her arm around his shoulder.

She looked up at Dev, her gaze beseeching. 'What happened here?'

'I'm quitting uni, Mum,' he said. 'I'm an actor.' His whole face ached as he spoke, but the words were strong and clear.

'That's a dream, not a career.' His dad didn't say the words, he spat them out.

'It's what I want.' What he needed to do.

'I won't support you, Devlin. I won't stand by and watch you fail—'

'I know that,' he interrupted. How well he knew that.

That his family wouldn't support him. That not one of them believed he'd succeed.

'Good,' his dad said. 'Then leave. You're not welcome here.'

It didn't surprise him. It had been coming for so long. His mum, the only reason he'd stayed, looked stricken.

He nodded. Then walked back up the hall the way he'd come.

He didn't say a word. No dramatic farewell. No parting words.

But he knew he'd never be back.

Graeme slowed to a stop at a paddock gate before a security guard waved them through. A dirt track wound its way over the smallest of hills, and then they were amongst the trailers that sprawled across Unit Base. The set was vast—yesterday the producer had told him it was the corner of a working sheep and canola farm. It spread across the almost perfectly flat countryside, overlooked by an irregular ridge of mountains. Yesterday, Dev's gaze had explored a landscape dotted with eucalyptus, rectangular fields of lurid yellow canola and paddocks desperately trying to hold onto winter hints of green. Today it was just a blur.

But something caught his eye as Graeme parked beside his trailer. Through the car window he followed that splash of colour with his eyes.

A woman in a bright blue dress, more like an oversized jumper, really, was barrelling rapidly along the path towards him. She was unmistakeable, her mop of choppy blonde hair shining like pale gold in the sun.

Ruby Bell.

She'd slipped his mind as soon as his nightly battle for sleep had begun, but now she'd sprung right back to the front, in full Technicolor.

He knew what she was: a distraction. A temporary focus.

But one he needed.

He was here. And thanks to Graeme—via Veronica—he'd be here on set each day, right on time. But right now he couldn't make himself care about the film, about his role.

Oh, he'd perform, right on cue, and to the best of his ability—as much as he was capable of, anyway.

But he wouldn't care. Couldn't care. Any more.

How was that for irony?

With his death, his father had—finally—got his way.

He was on time—just.

Ruby watched as he got out of the car, all loose-limbed and casual.

In contrast, she felt as stiff as a board. She kept making herself take deep, supposedly calming breaths as she gripped the papers in her hand, and reminding herself that she could do this—that this was her job.

It was just incredibly unfortunate it was *her* job. She shouldn't have been surprised, really, when Paul had taken her aside this morning and made her task clear: keep Dev on time and on schedule.

All the Dev-related rumours—a new one this morning hinting at a lot more than tardiness—should've made Paul's request a no-brainer.

Yet, she'd actually *gasped* when Paul had told her, and then had to make up some unfortunate lie about swallowing a fly, accompanied with much poorly acted faux coughing.

Once *again* Dev had managed to short-circuit her brain.

Because the task of babysitting talent was a perfectly typical request for the production co-ordinator, who, amongst other things, was responsible for organising actors' lives while on location.

Actors were notoriously unreliable. Putting together the call sheet was one thing—having anyone actually stick to it was something else entirely.

As she watched Dev watch her, a hip propped against his car, it was suddenly clear that getting him to do anything—at all—that she wanted could prove difficult.

This was not the man who'd smiled at her in the Lucyville pub last night, or who'd teased her on the street. Neither was he the man with the smug expression and the coffee stains on his shirt.

This man was completely unreadable.

'Good morning!' she managed, quite well, she thought.

He nodded sharply.

She thrust the portion of the script he'd be rehearsing today in his direction. 'Here are today's sides,' she said.

He took them from her with barely a glance. It was as if he was waiting for something—to figure something out.

'And?' he asked.

'I'll be taking you to be fitted by Costume, first,' she said. 'Then Hair and Make-up would like to see you prior to your rehearsal.'

'And you'll be escorting me?'

Ruby swallowed. 'Yes. I'll be looking after you today.'

It was immediately obvious that was the wrong thing to say. Something flickered in his gaze.

'I have my call sheet. I know where I need to be. I don't require hand-holding.'

'Paul asked that I...'

His glare told her that was another mistake, so she let the words drift off.

Then tried again. 'Mr Cooper, I'm here to help you.'

Somehow, those words changed everything, as if she'd flicked a switch. From defensive, and shuttered, his expression was suddenly...*considering?*

But Ruby didn't think for a moment that he'd simply accepted she was just doing her job. This was different—more calculating.

'Here to help,' he said to himself, as if he was turning the words over in his head.

Then he smiled, a blinding, movie-star smile.

And Ruby had absolutely no idea what had just happened.

It was dumb—really dumb—that he was surprised.

Heck—if *he* were the producer on this film, he'd have done the same thing.

It didn't mean he had to be happy about it.

He'd never been this kind of actor before; he'd never needed to be led around on some imaginary leash. Lord—he'd thought Graeme was bad enough.

And, of course, it had to be Ruby in charge of him.

It was a total waste of her time, of course. On set, he *was* fine, and not the fine he told himself he was whenever he was convincing himself to fall asleep.

He followed just slightly behind her. She was talking, quite rapidly, but he really wasn't paying much attention.

She was nervous, for sure. He *did* like that.

And he *did* like how the tables had turned. Last night she'd called the shots. Today—it was him.

Juvenile? Yes.

Fun? He thought so.

So Paul thought he needed looking after? No problem.

He'd be that actor, then. The ridiculous type who wanted everything in their trailer periwinkle blue, or who would only drink a particular brand of mineral water—not available locally, of course.

He'd prove Paul right—and irritate the self-important producer in the process.

A small win.

And it would push Ruby's buttons too—trigger that flare of response he'd already witnessed a handful of times, and was eager to experience again.

Dev smiled, just as Ruby stopped before a hulking white trailer and turned to face him.

Her forehead wrinkled as she studied him, as if she knew something was up.

He just smiled even more broadly.

Yes, this was an *excellent* idea.

Completely focused on the email she was reading—Arizona's agent, confirming that his client was available to attend an opening in Sydney the following week—Ruby picked up her loudly ringing phone from her overflowing desk without glancing at the screen.

'Ruby Bell.'

'Ruby.' A pause. 'Good afternoon.'

There was no point pretending she didn't recognise that voice. Her disloyal body practically shivered in recognition.

'How can I help, Mr Cooper?' she asked with determined brightness, her eyes not wavering from her laptop screen, although the email's words and sentences had somehow become an indecipherable alphabet jumble.

Even so, she tapped randomly on her keyboard. For her benefit, mostly, a reminder that she was a busy film professional who received phone calls from famous actors All The Time. She was working. This was her job.

No need for her mouth to go dry or for her cheeks to warm.

'Well,' he said, 'I have a problem.'

'Yes?' she prompted, with some trepidation.

He'd been scrupulously polite this morning. Allowed her to take him from appointment to appointment. He'd chatted inanely about the weather, and charmed every person she introduced him to.

But...

Occasionally he'd slant a glance in her direction that meant... she had absolutely no idea.

It wasn't about last night any more. She was sure. No question he'd long lost interest in perfectly average Ruby Bell by now.

Definitely.

'I can't figure out how to use the wireless Internet in my cottage.'

Oh. Her skin went hotter. Of course his phone call had nothing to do with her. *Of course it didn't.*

Hadn't she told him—what, three hours ago?—to call her any time?

Ruby took a deep breath. She really needed to pull herself together.

'I'm sorry to hear that, Mr Cooper,' she replied. 'I'll get that sorted for you straight away.'

'Appreciate it,' he said, and then the phone went silent.

Carefully, she placed her phone back onto her desk, darting her gaze about the room. She half expected everyone to be staring at her, to *know* exactly how flustered she was, despite all her efforts to not be. To somehow *know* that Dev had all but propositioned her outside the salubrious Lucyville Motel, even though she'd told her intrigued friends she hadn't seen Dev after she'd left the pub last night.

To *know* that chaperoning Dev around set this morning was stupidly difficult, despite her constant mental reminders that it was *so not a big deal,* and that she *was a professional* and *they were both adults* who could work together professionally despite the running-into-him thing, or the not-recognising-him thing, or saying-no-to-the-most-eligible-bachelor-in-the-world thing.

But no. Rohan worked quietly at his desk. Cath stood in front of the large whiteboard calendar, studying it with fierce concentration and a marker in her hand. Selena wasn't even in the room—she was out, busily signing in extras.

Ruby bit back a sigh. She was being ridiculous.

So she tilted her head left to right, rolled her shoulders a few times, wriggled her toes—and told herself she was cool, and calm and collected. *She was!*

And then she got back to work.

Less than an hour later, Dev stepped out onto the deck at the back of his cottage, sliding shut the glass door firmly behind him. Inside, one of the more junior members of the production office was busily fixing his 'broken' Internet.

He pressed his phone to his ear.

'Ruby Bell,' she said when she answered, sounding as brisk and polite as she had earlier.

'Ms Bell,' he said, ever so politely, 'thank you. I now have Internet.'

Well, he would once the guy inside realised the router had been unplugged.

'Oh, good,' she said. There was a beat or two of silence, and then she added, 'Can I help you with anything else?'

Dev's lips curled upwards.

'Yes, actually. I need a new hire car.'

'Is something wrong with your current car?' she asked.

No. Assuming you disregarded the fact that he had Graeme-the-warden driving him everywhere. Dev's suggestion he drive himself to set from now on was not warmly received. If Dev had access to the keys he never would've asked at all.

That would've made Veronica happy. About as happy as she'd been in her email this morning, and her many missed calls on his phone.

Turned out Graeme had passed on his trip to the pub.

Security—my arse.

'My current car is too...' he paused, as if in deep contemplation '...*feminine.*'

'Pardon me?'

'Too *feminine,*' he repeated.

The line remained silent. Was Ruby smiling? Frowning?

'I see,' she said, after a while. 'I'm sorry you find your *black four-wheel drive* so unsuitable. Can you explain to me what it is that you dislike about the car?'

There was nothing overtly discourteous in her tone—quite the opposite, in fact. Yet Dev heard the subtlest of subtle bites. He liked it.

'It's the upholstery,' he said. 'It has pink thread in it.'

'Ah,' she said, as if this were actually a valid complaint. 'Fair enough. Don't worry, I'll have a new car to you by tonight.'

'At the latest,' he said, just like one of the many delusionally self-important actors he knew who made these types of requests.

'Not a problem, Mr Cooper.'

'Appreciated, Ms Bell.'

Then he hung up with a smile on his face.

Ruby sat alone in her office, the Top 40 show on the radio her only company. It was late—really late, and she'd sent everyone else home fifteen minutes earlier.

But she had to get everything done—well, an hour ago, really—but Dev had really screwed up her day.

Losing Rohan for an hour to fix Dev's wireless had meant she'd had to run the call sheet alone; and unfortunately the runner she'd assigned to sort out the new hire car was young, and new, and seemed to ask Ruby a question every five minutes. Then, of course, there'd been Dev's email, asking for directions to every amenity in Lucyville. After she'd gritted her teeth and carefully replied to it—and therefore losing another thirty minutes—he'd blithely replied with one word: *Thanks.*

Thanks!

She'd silently screamed.

She'd had no idea Dev was like this—normally talent of the high-maintenance variety came with clear advance warning via the industry grapevine. Put two people who worked in film together, and guaranteed that stuff like 'Dev-Cooper-thought-his-car-was-too-girly' got talked about.

But—until the last twenty-four hours—she'd never heard a negative word about Devlin Cooper.

Oohing and ahhing about how he was *just* as gorgeous in real life—which she now knew to be true—yes, she'd heard that. But unreasonable, prima-donna carryings-on? Not a whisper.

Her phone rang, vibrating against the pile of sides—the scenes being filmed the next day—it rested upon.

Of course it was Dev, and reluctantly Ruby swiped her finger across the screen to answer the call.

'Mr Cooper,' Ruby said, setting the phone to loudspeaker so she could continue to work on the latest updates to a transport schedule. She was *not* going to let Dev distract her. 'How can I help you?'

'I was wondering,' he said, not sounding at all apologetic for calling so late, 'if you could recommend anywhere good to eat in Sydney.'

Ruby's jaw clenched. *Really?*

'Was it for a particular occasion?'

'A date,' he said. 'This weekend.'

Ruby determinedly ignored that irrational, disappointed kick she felt in her belly.

'Sure,' she managed to squeeze out. 'I'll get someone onto that for you tomorrow.'

'But I was hoping you could offer some personal recommendations.'

Had his voice become slightly deeper? More intimate?

Don't be an idiot! She typed the words on screen for good measure; maybe *then* it would sink in.

'Well,' she said, 'if you were thinking fine dining, then you probably can't go wrong with *Tetsuya's,* on Kent Street. Or *Quay,* at The Rocks.'

'Personal favourites?'

'No. I've heard the food is amazing, but I generally prefer somewhere a little less formal. Where people talk and laugh loudly and you don't need to book months in advance. You know?' Immediately she realised what she'd said. 'Although I'd imagine you don't have too many problems with getting a table.'

'Not usually,' he said, a smile in his voice. 'So where would *you* go for dinner this Saturday night in Sydney?'

She'd grown up in the outer suburbs of Sydney, but as an adult she'd spent little time there—aside from when she was working. And with twelve-to-fourteen-hour days typical on a film set, dining out—fine or otherwise—wasn't exactly a regular occurrence. Although, she'd crashed in the spare room of a set dresser between jobs last year...

'Some friends took me to a French Bistro right in the CBD when I was last in Sydney. It's a little fancy, but still relaxed. Plus, the Bombe Alaska is to die for.'

'Perfect. Would you be able to book me a table?'

Ruby gritted her teeth. *So not my job!*

'Sure!' she said, instead, with determined enthusiasm.

'Appreciate it,' he said, and the words were just as annoying the third time she'd heard them that day.

Then he hung up.

Ruby told herself she'd imagined the beginnings of a laugh before the phone went silent. As otherwise she'd need to drive to his place right now. And strangle him.

The next day was overcast, with rain forecast for the early afternoon.

Consequently, Asha, the second assistant director, was rather frantic when she rushed into Ruby's office just after eleven a.m.

'I need your help,' she said, running a hand through her shiny black bob. 'We have a situation in Hair and Make-up. Dev won't let anyone cut his hair, and we need him on set like *now*. We need to get this scene before the weather hits.'

Ruby sighed. She'd left him with hair and make-up not even

twenty minutes ago…but still—she really shouldn't be surprised.

A minute later, both women were striding across Unit Base.

'Dev isn't at all like what I expected,' Ruby said. She wrapped her arms tightly around herself as she walked, the breeze sharp through the thin cotton of her cardigan.

'You mean the whole "haven't slept or eaten in a month" thing?' Asha asked. 'Thank God Make-up and Wardrobe can work miracles is all I can say.' Then a long pause, and a conspiratorial whisper: 'I hear that he's nursing a broken heart. That Estelle van der something? She's already hooked up with someone new. Poor guy.'

Poor guy? Right.

'Yeah, that, I guess,' Ruby said. 'But I meant all of his demands? It's driving me nuts.'

Asha shot her a surprised glance. 'Really? Honestly, up until just now he's been a model actor. It's amazing how quickly he's learnt his scenes and he just nailed our rehearsals yesterday. His professionalism is the only reason we can shoot anything today.'

Ruby slowed her pace slightly. 'No complaints about his costume? Requests for a box of chocolates with all the soft-centred ones removed?'

Both were the type of requests that the Dev she'd been dealing with over the past day and a half would *definitely* have asked. Just this morning he'd asked to have new curtains installed in his trailer, as the current set let in too much light when closed. *Apparently.* Then he'd asked for a very specific selection of organic fruit. Rohan was wasting his time on that, right now. Ugh!

'No,' Asha said, coming to a halt outside the hair and make-up trailer. 'This random hair thing is it. But, it's only been a couple of days. Maybe he'll reveal his true self to all of us on set soon.'

'Hmm,' was all that Ruby could say to that. A niggling suspicion that she'd dismissed as ridiculous, impossible, was now niggling, well…louder.

But surely he wouldn't…?

She opened the door to the trailer, taking in the frustrated-looking hair stylist and his assistant—and of course Dev, sprawled ever-so-casually in front of a mirror, complete with two days' worth of—she had to admit—sexy stubble. As she stepped inside he met her gaze in the glass.

And winked.

Ruby dug her fingernails into her palms, then took a deep, calming breath. The action was not soothing in the slightest, but it did help her speak in a fair facsimile of an I've-got-everything-under-control production co-ordinator.

'Could I have a few minutes with Mr Cooper?'

It was a perfectly reasonable request—it was her job to fix exactly these types of hiccups—and so with quick nods and hopeful expressions aimed in Ruby's direction everyone filed out.

Ever so slowly—and Ruby now *knew* he was enjoying this—Dev spun his chair around to face her. His assessing gaze travelled over her, from her flat, knee-high leather boots, up to her fitted navy jeans, cream tank top and oversized, over-long wool cardigan. Then to her face—touching on her lips, her eyes, her hair.

Ruby wanted to kick herself for being pleased she'd made an effort with her make-up today. She'd done so yesterday too, not letting herself acknowledge until just now that it had—of course—been for Devlin Cooper.

God, she frustrated herself. She'd been sure she'd long ago got past this—this pathetic need for male attention. The need for anyone else to provide her with validation, other than herself.

No. That hadn't changed.

He opened his mouth, guaranteed to say something teasing and clever. He had that look in his eyes—she'd seen it in his movies, and definitely in person.

She didn't give him the chance.

'Who the *hell* do you think you are?'

Ruby had the satisfaction of watching his eyes widen in surprise. But he recovered quickly, as smooth as silk. 'I believe I'm Devlin Cooper.' He shrugged. 'You know, the actor?'

She shook her head. 'No way. Don't be smart. I'm onto you.'

'*Onto* me?' he asked, raising an eyebrow. 'What exactly are you *onto?*'

Ruby bit her lip, trying to hold onto the barest thread of control. Could he be any more deliberately oblivious? Any more *arrogant?*

'This,' she said, throwing her arms up to encompass the trailer. 'And the phone calls, the emails, the hire car, the chocolates, the fruit, the curtains...' Ruby started to count them off on her fingers. 'What next? What next trivial, unreasonable task are you going to lob in my direction?'

'You don't feel my requests are legitimate?' he asked. If he was at all bothered by her rapidly rising voice, his expression revealed nothing.

'I know they're not.' She glared at him when he tried to speak again. 'And I don't care why you've been doing it: I don't care if you're so shocked by the concept of a woman saying no to you that you need to be as irritating as possible in revenge, but—*please*—just stop.'

Dev blinked. 'Is that what you think I'm doing?' In contrast to even a moment before, now he looked dumbfounded—his forehead wrinkled in consternation. 'That's not it at all.'

But she was barely listening now.

'In case you're not aware, when you pull stunts like this, Paul—you know, my boss?—expects me to sort it all immediately. If I don't—if filming is held up, if we can't shoot a scene because of you, or if I need to ask Paul to call your agent to kick your butt into gear—it isn't *you* who looks like a massive, unprofessional loser. *It's me.*'

Dev pushed himself to his feet. He was in costume: dark brown trousers, a soft tan shirt with the sleeves rolled up, a heavy leather belt and holster, plus chunky work boots—he was playing an early nineteen hundreds Australian drover after all. Temporarily, her tirade was clogged in her throat as she digested the sight of him approaching her. He was so tall, so broad—and suddenly the trailer felt so small.

But then her frustration bubbled over again. Hot, famous movie star or not—*nobody* got away with treating Ruby Bell this way.

'You might have forgotten what it's like to rely on a regular salary, but trust me—I haven't. And I'm not having some entitled, full-of-himself actor think it's okay to stomp all over my reputation, my professionalism, my...'

With every word her voice became higher and less steady.

Dev had stopped in front of her. Not close enough to crowd her, not at all, and yet she found that words began to escape her as he studied her, his gaze constant, searching and...what? Not arrogant. Not angry. Not even shocked...

Sad? No, not that either. But it wasn't what she expected.

It had been silent for long seconds, and Ruby swallowed, trying to pull herself together.

'If you don't stop,' she began, 'I'll...'

And here her tirade came to its pathetic—and now clearly obvious—end.

What exactly would she do? What could she do? She'd just told him that she'd get blamed for any problems he caused, and that was pretty much true. And it wasn't as if she could get him fired.

Hmm. Let me think: Easily replaceable production co-ordinator versus the man who's starred in the world's highest grossing spy franchise?

She tangled her fingers into the fabric of her cardigan, suddenly needing to hold onto something.

Oh, God. What had she done? All he had to do was complain to Paul and...

Dev was still watching her.

'You'll what, Ruby?'

She made herself meet his gaze. 'I—' she started. She should apologise, she knew. Grovel, even—do anything to patch up the past few minutes as if they had never, ever happened.

But she couldn't do it—it would be like time-travelling ten years into her past.

'I'd *appreciate it*,' she said, deliberately mimicking him, 'if you could carefully consider your future requests, or issues, before contacting myself, or my office. We're all very busy at the moment.'

Even that was far from an appropriate request to make of a film's biggest star, but she just *couldn't* concede any less.

In response, Dev smiled. The sudden lightness in his gaze made Ruby's heart skip a beat. Alone in a room with Dev Cooper, Ruby would challenge any woman not to do the same—irritated beyond belief or not.

'It wasn't revenge,' he said, simply.

'But it was something,' Ruby prompted. What was all this about?

'I'm sorry that you thought I was trying to make you look bad in front of your boss and colleagues. I can assure you I wasn't.'

Even knowing he was a very good actor, Ruby believed him. Those eyes, in real life, were *nothing at all* like what you saw on celluloid. They revealed so much more—more than Ruby could even begin to interpret.

'It's much simpler than that. Much less exciting than some dastardly vengeful plan.'

Ruby crossed her arms, watching him stonily.

He sighed. 'Okay, bad joke. Look…' He looked down at the trailer floor for just a moment. 'It's simple, really. I don't need "looking after".'

Ruby narrowed her eyes. 'And the fact I'm the brunt of this behaviour is an unfortunate coincidence?'

'No,' he conceded. 'I just like…' He studied her face, then focused on her eyes, as if he was trying to work something out. 'I like seeing you react.'

She was not deluded enough to think that she stood out amongst all the other women she *knew* he surrounded himself with. She'd seen the photos of him with Estelle—a *supermodel,* for crying out loud. This juvenile game had *nothing* to do with her. Not really.

This was about his ego, his sense of the way things should be.

She didn't come into it at all.

Ruby spoke very politely. 'Please carefully consider your future requests, or issues, before contacting myself, or my office,' she repeated.

He nodded, and for the first time in long minutes Ruby felt as if she was breathing normally.

'I'll do my best,' he said.

Every muscle in her body that had begun to relax re-tightened, ready for battle. Had he not heard a word she'd said? How could he possibly think—?

'No more stunts like this—I get it. I won't impact the filming schedule.'

But...

He grinned, but that brightness she'd seen—just for that moment—had long disappeared. Now there was a heaviness to his gaze, and the lines around his mouth were tight.

'I think I'm having too much fun with you.'

'I'm not interested,' she said, quick as a flash. But they both heard that she didn't really believe that.

Since when had she been this transparent?

He was so sure he knew where this was headed it made her want to scream. And simultaneously made her question her sanity. There was just something about the man, and the way he looked at her, that had her questioning herself. Had her questioning the rules she'd laid down for herself long ago...

She shook her head firmly.

'I'm going to tell Hair and Make-up that it was a misunderstanding and you're happy to go with the haircut as planned.'

He nodded sharply.

She turned to go, but paused at the trailer door.

'You do realise that the kid who threw sticks at the girl he liked in primary school never did get the girl?'

He laughed, the deep sound making her shiver. 'Not in my experience.'

Ruby slammed the door behind her as she left.

CHAPTER FOUR

'RUBY, CAN I HAVE a minute?'

Paul spoke from the hallway, barely poking his head into the busy office. He didn't bother waiting for an answer—as of course it wasn't a question—and so half a minute later Ruby was closing the door behind her as she stepped into the producer's office.

'Yes?'

Paul was rubbing his forehead, which wasn't a good sign.

'Are the drivers organised for tomorrow night?' he asked.

Paul was attending the premiere of his latest film in Sydney. Both Dev and Arizona would also be walking the red carpet— a bit of extra attention for that film, plus some early promo for *The Land.* 'Of course. All three cars are sorted.'

As was contractually necessary. *Must travel in own car* was a pretty standard condition for most actors. Quite the contrast to Ruby, who had driven up to Lucyville with her hire car packed full with everything she owned, Rohan *and* one of the girls from Accounts. Plus some miscellaneous lighting equipment.

Paul nodded sharply. 'Good, good.'

Then he went silent, allowing Ruby to start dreaming up all the potential reasons why he'd *really* needed to talk to her.

Right at the top of that list was Dev.

'So. I hear you had some luck talking Dev around, yesterday.'

Got it in one.

'Yes,' she said, far more calmly than she felt. 'He just needed a little time to understand what was required.'

'Excellent,' Paul said. 'As unfortunately neither his agent or I are having much luck making him *understand* that he signed a contract that specified he walk the red carpet at this premiere. He's refusing to go.'

Of course he was.

Ruby bit back a sigh. 'I don't think I'd have any more chance of talking him around than you would.'

'I have faith in you.'

Which meant: *Go fix this, Ruby.*

Paul had already reached for his phone, casually moving on to his next production crisis, now that—in his mind at least—this particular issue was sorted.

So Ruby walked out of his office, down the hallway, outside onto the dusty grass, then all the way across Unit Base to where the opulent, shiny black actors' trailers that housed Arizona and Dev were situated.

And knocked, very loudly, on Dev's door.

He was, Dev decided, becoming quite accustomed to people being annoyed with him.

There was Veronica, of course, all but breathing fire across the cellular network whenever she called. Her multiple-times-a-day tirades were exclusively for the benefit of his voicemail, however, as Dev considered Graeme a sufficient conduit for anything that Veronica really needed to know. He figured his agent could hardly complain. She'd planted her security guy/minder/driver/spy—she might as well get her money's worth.

Or, more accurately, *his* money's worth. As of course that was what all this was about—Veronica's much-stated concern for him was all about the money. He was her biggest star, and now she was panicking.

But he felt no guilt. He'd made Veronica very, very rich. He owed her nothing.

Then there was Graeme. The director. The producer. The rest of the crew. He gave them all just exactly what was needed—

whether it be his acting skills, the answer to a question, or simple conversation. But not one skerrick more.

Then his mother had started calling. In her first voice message, she explained she'd heard on the news that he was in
Australia, and was hoping they could catch up.

He'd meant to call her, but then didn't. Couldn't.

And she'd kept calling, kept leaving polite, friendly messages, that always ended with a soft *love you.*

Each call made him feel like something you'd scrape off your
boot, but, as he'd been doing lately, he just shoved that problem
aside. To worry about later. Eventually…

Most likely at three in the morning, when he was so overwhelmed with exhaustion that he could no longer ignore the
thoughts that caused him pain.

He clenched his jaw. *No.*

The woman on the other side of his trailer door, *she* was
who he needed to be thinking about. Somehow, randomly, she'd
grabbed his attention. With her, he forgot all the other rubbish
that was cluttering up his head.

And she was, unquestionably, very, very annoyed with him.

He smiled, and walked to the door.

He opened the door mid-knock, triggering a surprised, 'Oh!'
and she stumbled a step inside.

He didn't step back himself, forcing her to squeeze past
him. Not quite close enough for their bodies to touch, but close
enough that her clothes brushed against his.

Yes, he was being far from a gentleman, but no—he didn't
care.

He found himself craving that flare in Ruby's gaze, that look
she worked so hard to disguise.

But it was there—this heat between them. He knew it, she
knew it—she just needed to get over whatever ridiculous imagined rules she'd created in her head and let the inevitable happen.

He let the trailer door swing shut behind him and turned
to face her. She walked right into the middle of his trailer, in
the 'living' section of the luxury motorhome. The trailer was

practically soundproof, so now they both stood, looking at each other, in silence.

That didn't last long.

'I thought I made myself clear,' she said, frustration flooding her voice, 'how important my career is to me, and how you have *no right* to mess with it. To mess with my life.'

'But I haven't.'

She blinked. 'What would you call this? Refusing to attend a premiere that's in your contract?'

'Have I held up filming? Have I embarrassed you professionally?'

'You will if you don't go,' she said simply.

He smiled. 'Then you just need to get me to go.'

Her eyes narrowed. 'How?'

'Dinner.'

He hadn't planned this. Hadn't planned anything beyond saying no to Paul and seeing what happened next.

With Ruby there wasn't a script—things just happened.

But dinner, suddenly, was the perfectly obvious solution.

'That's blackmail,' she said, with bite.

He shrugged. 'Yes.'

No, he most definitely was *not* a gentleman.

She sighed loudly and rubbed her hands up and down her arms. 'So if I agree to dinner, you'll attend the premiere.' It wasn't a question.

'And make you look like a miracle-worker in front of your producer.'

She rolled her eyes. 'I'd rather you'd just gone to the premiere and never brought me into this at all.' She paused, meeting his gaze.

Her expression was sharp and assessing. 'Dinner at that French bistro on Saturday night—you booked that for…whatever *this* is.'

Maybe he had? At the time it'd been about riling her up, teasing her, irritating her with the idea he had a date with another woman. Childish, but he hadn't had a plan. Not consciously, anyway.

'Yes,' he said, because he knew she'd hate that answer.

'God, you're so, so sure of yourself, aren't you?'

He didn't bother replying. Instead he walked past her, then settled himself onto one of the small navy-blue couches. 'Why don't you take a seat? We can work out the details of our date.'

'No, thank you,' she said, very crisply. 'I need to get back to the office. I don't have time during my workday to waste on this. Call me later. Or even better, email me. More efficient.'

Lord, he liked her. So direct. So to the point.

She spun on her booted heel, then paused mid-spin.

'So this is your way of maintaining your one-hundred-percent never-rejected perfect score or something?'

'You can think of it that way if you like.'

She groaned. 'You think you're very clever, don't you?'

Considering he'd just achieved exactly what he wanted, he didn't consider it necessary to reply to this question either.

She continued her exit, but at the door she, just as he expected, had to deliver a final parting shot. Just as she had yesterday.

'You know what, Mr Cooper? Everything I'd heard about you before this week was good. Glowing even. Everyone likes you. Everyone loves to work with you. So, I reckon you must *really* be a great actor. Because, quite frankly, I don't think you're a very nice person.'

This time he had no pithy retort, so he just let her go.

After all, she was partly right. Right now he didn't feel like the Dev that everyone liked, as she said. The Dev that loved his job and that was beloved of many a film crew. The Dev with a million friends and a lifestyle that most could only dream of.

Right now he didn't know what type of person he was at all.

Ruby had laid out every single item of clothing she owned on her motel-room bed. Not just the clothing she'd brought with her for this film—everything she owned.

Years ago she'd got into the routine of selling her clothes before departing for a job overseas—eBay was brilliant for that purpose—rather than lugging it with her across the world.

She'd always thought it rather a flawless plan. She had a keen eye for an online shopping bargain, so she was rarely out of pocket, and, more importantly, she had the perfect excuse to buy an entirely new, season-appropriate wardrobe every six months or so.

The rare occasions she did date, it was always between films, so having a favourite, guaranteed-to-feel-awesome-in outfit was not really all that essential. She knew well in advance if she had a premiere to attend, so she could plan ahead—and besides, the full-length formal gowns were really only for the talent at those events, not the crew.

So. Consequently here she was, hands on hips—and not far from putting her head in her hands—with absolutely nothing to wear on her date with Dev.

It was tempting, really, *really* tempting, to rock up for her date in jeans and a ratty old T-shirt. So her clothing choice would make a very obvious statement about how she felt about the whole situation.

But, unfortunately, she just couldn't.

Turned out she was—much to her despair—incapable of being truly cool, and strong, and defiant. In this way, at least. Nope. Just as she'd been agonising over her clothing choices for work each day, she wanted to look her best on Saturday night.

Yes, it was pathetic. Yes, it didn't say a lot for her that, despite Dev's ridiculous manipulating of her and their situation, she still felt her body react at even the *thought* of him. And when they were together...well.

But then, he *was* basically the sexiest man on earth. She shouldn't be too hard on herself. Surely she wouldn't be human if she didn't wonder...

It was just a little galling to realise that she—who did know better—could still be distracted by looks over personality. As, really, there wasn't a whole lot about Devlin Cooper for her to like right now.

A long time ago, the Devlin Coopers of the world had been her type. Not that she had a life populated with movie stars, but at high school she'd gone for the captain of the footy team. And the captain of the tennis team. And the very charismatic head boy who every girl had been in love with. Then once she left school, it was the sexy bartender. Or the hot lawyer who ordered a latte every morning at the café where she worked. Or the son of the owner of the café. And...*and, and, and...*

She'd search out the hottest guy, the most popular guy, the guy who was the absolute least attainable for a girl like her—the rebellious foster child, abandoned by her teenage mother, with a reputation a mile long.

And then she would make it her mission to get him.

It was all about her goal, her goal to get the guy, to have him want her—*her*—Ruby Bell, who was *nobody.* Not popular, not unpopular. Not the prettiest, not the least attractive. And when she got him—and she nearly always did—she had that night, or nights, or maybe only a few hours, where she got to feel beautiful and desirable and valued and *wanted.*

But of course that feeling didn't last. She—and her temporary value—was inevitably dropped. She'd hurt and cry and feel just as worthless as she had before that perfect, gorgeous guy had kissed her.

Then the cycle would start again.

Ruby's eyes stung, and she realised she was on the verge of tears. Another memory—one that came later—was threatening, right at the edges of her subconscious.

But she wasn't going there—not tonight, and not because of Dev.

What was important was that she'd turned her life around. Never again would she need a man to make her feel alive—to feel worthy. Never again would she be sweet, and obliging and void of any opinion purely for the attention and approval of another person.

And never again would she be the girl that was whispered about. Who walked into a room only to have the men study her with questions in their eyes—and the women with daggers in theirs.

She'd grown up in a swirl of gossip and speculation, and her adult life had begun that way too—and way too early.

The sad thing was, at first she'd actually liked the attention. She wasn't the shy girl at the back of the classroom, she was a girl who people talked about, who people noticed. Suddenly *everyone* knew her name.

Maybe at first she'd fuelled the gossip. She'd been increasingly outrageous, telling herself she was in control, inwardly laughing at the people who looked at her with such disdain.

But at some point the power had shifted.

Or maybe she'd just never had any power at all.

Now she was all grown up. She was twenty-nine years old. She no longer needed anyone to validate her. She no longer harboured a fear it had taken her years to acknowledge—that if her mother hadn't wanted her, then maybe no one ever would. In men and their fleeting attention she'd received the attention and the *wanting* she'd so badly craved.

But now she knew she didn't need a man. She had her career, and her friends, and a lifestyle that she adored. If she dated, she chose men who were the opposite to the high-school football stars and Devlin Coopers of the world. And it was never for very long.

She was always in control. Everything was perfect.

And another beautiful man was not going to change any of that. She would not slide into habits long severed, or let their date impact her professional reputation: she had never been, and would never be, the subject of gossip at work. Gossip would never colour her decisions—would never control her—ever again.

She didn't hide her past from anyone—but it was the *past*. She couldn't let herself head down that path again. To lose herself while wanting something a man could never give her.

Ruby needed only herself. Could rely, *only,* on herself.

She turned, and flopped onto her back on her bed, uncaring of the clothing she squashed and creased beneath her.

Hmm. That was all well and good—and *right.*

But.

She still had a date with Devlin Cooper in two days' time.

An emergency shopping expedition was—most definitely—required.

Ruby had to spend a few hours in the office on Saturday morning, and so by the time she'd driven the four hours into the city, she was cutting it extremely fine.

Fortunately, one of her good friends was between films at the moment. So she was meeting Gwen, an exceedingly glamorous costume designer, at a boutique in Paddington, rather than hitting the department stores in a fit of mad desperation.

As she stepped into the store, complete with its crystal chandeliers, chunky red leather armchairs and modern, smooth-edged white shelving, Gwen squealed and trotted towards her on towering platform heels.

'Ruby! It's been for ever!' she announced as she wrapped her into a hug.

She'd considered sharing the identity of her date with Gwen, but had decided, on balance, that it was best if she didn't. Yes, she trusted her friend, but…it really was better if no one knew. It was only one date, after all.

In the same vein, she'd taken steps to ensure—as much as was possible—that their date remained firmly under the radar. When Dev had called her—she'd known he wouldn't email—she'd made it very clear that the gorgeous French bistro she'd booked was no longer suitable. It was not the type of place where privacy—and a lack of photography—could be assured. The last thing she needed was some grainy photo snapped on someone's mobile phone making it onto Twitter and, eventually, to the film set.

Yes, she was likely paranoid, and such a liaison with a film's star would not signal the end of her career. She *knew* that film sets could be the home to all sorts of flings and the more than occasional affair. It was natural in an industry where the majority of the crew were well under forty—the transient lifestyle was not ideal for anyone with a family, and roots.

She just didn't want to be that woman Dev had a fling with. She'd been *that woman* enough times in her life. Thank you very much.

So this was, she realised as Gwen unhooked a dress from a shiny chrome rack to display to her, more about how she perceived herself than about how anyone else would perceive her.

Which really was just as important… No. More important than her professional reputation.

But she'd fiercely protect that, too.

'What do you think?' Gwen asked, giving the coat hanger a little shake so that the dress's delicate beading shimmered beneath the down lights.

It was a cocktail-length dress, in shades of green. On the hanger it looked like nothing but pretty fabric, but of course she tried it on.

Ruby was bigger than the average tiny actress that Gwen was used to dressing, but still—her friend certainly had an eye for what suited her body.

As she stepped out of the change room and in front of the mirror Ruby couldn't help but suck in a breath of surprise.

She looked…

'Beautiful!' Gwen declared happily. 'It's perfect.'

Ruby twisted from side to side, studying herself. The dress was gorgeous, with heavily beaded and embroidered cap sleeves and a sweetheart neckline that flattered her average-sized curves. The silk followed the curve of her waist and hips, ending well above her knee. The beading continued throughout the fabric, becoming sparser at her waist before ending in a shimmer of green and flecks of gold at the hem. It was simple—but not. Striking—but not glitzy.

She loved it.

Twenty minutes later she'd parted with a not insignificant portion of her savings, and headed with Gwen to find the perfect matching heels and a short, sexy, swingy jacket.

And an hour after that she was alone in the hotel room she'd booked, only a short walk from the crazily exclusive restaurant where she would be meeting Dev. Really soon.

The dress sparkled prettily on her bed. She had her make-up and the perfect shade of nail polish raring to go in the bathroom.

But she paused, rather than walking to the shower. She looked at herself reflected in the mirrored hotel wardrobe.

There she was, in jeans and hair that had transitioned from deliberately choppy to plain old messy at some point in the day.

She wouldn't say she lacked confidence in herself or her looks. She didn't think she was hideously *un*attractive, but... *really?* When Dev could have anyone, why her?

It must be the challenge. It could be nothing else. And maybe he felt that he should be the one doing the rejecting, not her?

She nodded, and she watched the movement reshuffle her hair just a little.

Yes. That was it.

And after tonight—that would be that. He'd have achieved his goal, and in a week's time she'd be very, very old news.

Which suited her just fine.

Didn't it?

CHAPTER FIVE

DEV WAS LATE. Only a few minutes, but late, just the same.

He'd meant to be later, actually, having liked the idea of Ruby sitting alone at the restaurant, getting increasingly frustrated with him.

Simply because he enjoyed the flash of anger in her eyes almost as much as the heat of the attraction she was so determinedly—and continually—ignoring.

But, after a while, he began to feel like a bit of an idiot sitting alone in his penthouse suite, mindlessly watching the Saturday night rugby, when the alternative was spending time with a beautiful...

No, not beautiful. At least not on the standards that Hollywood judged beauty. But a compelling...intriguing woman. Yes, she was that.

Unarguably more interesting than his own company.

But when he was ushered into the private dining area of the exclusive restaurant by an impeccably well-mannered maître d', he was met by a table exquisitely set for two—but no Ruby.

His lips quirked as he settled into his seat. *Interesting.*

The restaurant sat right on the edge of Circular Quay, its floor-to-ceiling windows forming a subtly curved wall that provided a spectacular view of the harbour. To the right were the dramatic sails of the opera house. Straight ahead was the incomparable harbour bridge. Lights illuminated the mammoth structure, highlighting its huge metal beams.

He'd eaten at this restaurant before, and had certainly dined against a backdrop of the world's most beautiful skylines many, many times—but he wouldn't be human if he wasn't impressed by sparkling Sydney by night.

It was like nowhere else in the world.

However. Sitting alone in a dining room that could seat thirty—and which he'd had organised for tonight to seat only two—even a remarkable view could quickly become boring.

Which it did.

A waiter came and offered him a taste of the wine he'd selected, then after pouring Dev's glass he merged once again, silently, into the background.

Minutes passed. Slowly, he assumed, as he refused to succumb and check his watch.

He considered—then dismissed—the possibility that she wasn't coming at all.

No, she'd be here.

Almost on cue, the door to the private room opened on whisper-smooth hinges. He looked up to watch Ruby being ushered inside. And then kept on looking.

She wore a dress in greens and gold that caught and reflected every bit of light in the room. Her legs were long beneath a skirt that hit at mid thigh, and shown off to perfection by strappy, criss-crossed heels. When his gaze—eventually—met hers, he connected with eyes that were defiant and bold beneath a fringe that was smoother and more perfect than usual: not a golden strand out of place.

Her lips curved in greeting, but he wouldn't call it a smile.

He stood as she approached the table, and she blinked a couple of times as he did so, her gaze flicking over him for the briefest of instants.

The maître d' received a genuine smile as he offered Ruby her seat, and he then launched into his spiel, speaking—Dev assumed—of wine and food, but he really wasn't paying any attention. Instead he took the opportunity to just look at Ruby as she tilted her chin upwards and listened attentively.

This was, after all, about the first time she'd been perfectly still, and silent, in his presence, since their original *interlude* beside the costume trailer.

Then, she'd been veering towards adorable, while tonight she was polished and perfect. Different, for sure—but equally appealing.

After a short conversation, the maître d' repeated his vanishing act, and Ruby turned her gaze onto him.

'You're late,' he pointed out.

She nodded. 'So were you.'

He smiled, surprised. 'How did you know?'

'I didn't. But it seemed the kind of stunt you would pull. You've been very consistent in your quest to irritate me.' Calmly, she reached for her water glass. 'Not very chivalrous of you, however.' Another pause. 'Personally, I am never—intentionally—less than punctual. Time is everything in my job, and I see no reason why it shouldn't be in the rest of my life.'

Time is everything.

How true. Often, Dev had only recently discovered, you had a lot less time than you thought.

'So chivalry is important to you, Ruby?'

She took a sip from her water glass, then studied him over the rim. 'Actually, no,' she replied, surprising him. She looked out towards the opera house, her forehead wrinkling slightly. 'I mean, of course being courteous and honourable or gallant—or whatever a chivalrous man is supposed to be—is important.' She gave him a look that underlined the fact she clearly considered him to be none of those things. 'But it has to be genuine. Standing up when I approach the table, for example—' her words were razor sharp '—is meaningless. It has to mean something—have a basis in respect—otherwise I'd really rather you didn't bother.'

'I respect you,' he said.

She laughed with not a trace of pretention. 'I find that very hard to believe.'

'It's the truth,' he said. He wasn't going to bother explaining himself, but then somehow found himself doing so anyway. 'I was late because I like seeing you react, not because I don't value you and your time. I apologise if you feel that way.'

'I'm sure you agree that distinction is impossible to make from my point of view.'

Dev almost, almost, felt bad about it—but not quite. He was enjoying this—enjoying her—too much.

'You like pushing my buttons,' she said. 'You're very good at it.'

He shrugged, studying her. 'So is that what you're looking for? An honourable, perfectly chivalrous specimen of a man?'

Dev knew he was not that man.

Immediately, she shook her head. 'Absolutely not. I'm looking for no man at all.'

'You're focusing on your career?'

Almost silently the maître d' reappeared and filled her wine glass.

'Yes, but that's not the reason. I don't need a man. At all.'

'Need, or want?'

She rolled her eyes dismissively. 'Neither.'

He considered this unexpected announcement as their entrées arrived, but he wasn't about to question her further. Tonight was not for detailed analysis of their respective relationship goals.

For the record, his was—and had always been—to have no relationship at all. Estelle had been an unexpected exception, a relationship that had evolved, at times—it seemed—almost without his participation. Yes, he'd liked her. Enjoyed his time with her. Maybe considered the idea that he loved her.

But that night she'd left, she'd made it crystal clear that what he felt wasn't love. How had she put it?

Love is when you share yourself—reveal yourself. Your thoughts, your feelings, your fears. Something. Everything! Not nothing. Not absolutely nothing.

At the time he hadn't questioned her. But later, when he'd asked himself that question—if that *was* what he'd done, and who he was—he couldn't disagree.

They ate their salmon for a while in silence, their knives scraping loudly on the fine bone china.

'Is this really what you wanted?' she asked. She was still focused on her meal, her eyes on her plate, not on him.

She meant this date, this time alone with her.

'Yes.'

Now she glanced up. The harder edge to her gaze from before was gone; now she just looked confused. 'Seriously? Why on earth would you want to spend an evening with a woman who doesn't particularly like you?'

'I thought you said you didn't know me well enough to dislike me.'

She raised an eyebrow. 'I've begun to revise that opinion.'

He smiled. Maybe something resembling his *famous Dev Cooper smile,* as he didn't miss the way her cheeks went pink, or how eager she was to look away.

'You like me.'

Instantly, she met his gaze. 'Here we go again. It's getting tedious. Why on earth should I like you?'

'I'm charming,' he said.

She snorted. 'What exactly is your definition of the word? Blackmailing a woman into dating you? Really?'

'No. I must admit this is not my standard dating procedure.'

'For the sake of the thousands of women you've ever dated, I'm relieved to hear that.'

'Not thousands,' he said.

She waved her wine glass in a gesture of dismissal. 'Hundreds, then.'

No, not that many either. In hindsight, maybe Estelle was not the first to observe his relationship failings. Or, more likely, she was the only one he'd allowed close enough to notice.

A mistake, clearly.

'I'm not—' he began, then stopped.

I'm not myself at the moment.

No, there was no need to say that to Ruby. That was the whole point, wasn't it? For Ruby to be his distraction?

'You're not what?' she asked.

He gave a little shake of his head. 'It doesn't matter. All that matters is that we're here now.' He leant back in his chair a little, studying her. 'We're here, in this amazing city, at this amazing restaurant. And you, Ruby Bell, are wearing one amazing dress.'

The pink to her cheeks escalated to a blush, but otherwise she gave no indication of being affected by his words.

'Thank you,' she said, just a little stiffly.

'Here's an idea,' he said. 'How about we call a truce? For tonight. For argument's sake, let's pretend you don't hate my guts, or the way we both came to be sitting together at this table.'

She grinned, then looked surprised that she had. 'I don't hate you,' she said. 'You just haven't given me a heck of a lot to like.'

'I'll try harder,' he promised.

She held his gaze for a long, long while. Considering his words.

'Okay,' she finally conceded. 'But just for tonight.'

Belatedly, Ruby acknowledged that her dessert plate was completely empty—excluding some melted remnants of sorbet. She could barely remember what it tasted like—she'd been so focused on their conversation.

How had this happened?

A couple of hours ago she'd been dreading this date…

No. That was clearly a lie. Anxiously anticipating was far more on the mark.

But now, she found herself in the midst of a really fantastic evening. *Date.* A date with a movie star.

Although, oddly, she found she needed to remind herself of that fact every now and again. A little mental pinch of her arm, so to speak.

He was different tonight. Only for a moment earlier, and even then she was unsure whether she'd imagined it, had his gaze darkened. She realised that up until tonight there had been a kind of shadow to Dev. A…burden, maybe?

But tonight he was different. There was more of an openness to his expression. Oddly, as they chatted—initially about the industry but then, thankfully, about basically everything but—Ruby had the sense that the shadow was gradually lifting. She found herself wanting to find opportunities to make him smile again, to laugh.

It was as if he was out of practice.

Ruby gave herself a mental shake.

Oh, no. Now *that* was wishful thinking. She was putting way too much thought into this.

She needed to keep this simple: it was a date. One date. Only.

They'd just finished trading stories of their varied travel disasters. She'd noticed that Dev hadn't spoken of *that time I was mobbed by fans in Paris* or *this one time I was invited for afternoon tea with the Queen*—it was as if he was distancing himself from what made him so, so different from her. Somehow, he was making himself relatable. A real person.

Was he doing it deliberately?

Yes, for sure. He'd been right before—he *was* charming, and smart.

But also…it was working. She found herself questioning her opinion of him. She'd certainly relaxed. Something she knew was unwise, but the wine, the food, the lighting, and Dev… yeah, Dev… It was…he was…pretty much an irresistible force.

But not quite.

'Why film production?' he asked, changing the direction of their conversation yet again.

Ruby swirled her Shiraz in its oversized glass. 'Would you believe I'm a failed actor?' she asked.

'Yes,' he said, immediately.

She raised her eyebrows. 'Is it that obvious?'

He nodded, assessing her. 'Acting requires a certain…artifice. You—you tell it how it is. You're not pretending, not hiding what you think.'

She shifted a little in her seat, uncomfortable. 'You're saying I'm tactless?' she said, attempting a teasing tone but failing.

'Honest,' he said, disagreeing with her.

His gaze had shifted a little, become more serious. He was watching her closely, and it left her feeling exposed. She didn't like it.

'But,' he said, 'sometimes you try to hide what you're not saying: frustration, dismissal...attraction.'

Ruby had a feeling she wasn't being as successful in that goal as she'd like tonight. What could he see in her expression?

She decided it best not to consider that at all.

'You're partly right,' she said. 'At school I loved to act, but really I was only playing variations of myself. I wasn't any good at stepping into another character.' She laughed. 'But I still wanted to work in film—you know, delusions of glamour— and I couldn't wait to travel the world—so, I went to uni, then started at the bottom and worked my way up.'

'You were good at school?'

She shook her head, laughing. 'Not at all. I went to uni when I was twenty, after going back to finish Year Twelve. I had a... rebellious phase, I'd guess you'd call it.'

Dev's eyebrows rose. 'Really?'

She smiled, pleased she'd surprised him. 'Most definitely. A combination of a few things, but mostly I think I was just a pretty unhappy teenager.' She paused, not sure how much to share. But then, it was no secret. 'I was a foster child, and ended up going through a few different families as a teenager. For some reason I just couldn't stay away from trouble.'

He just nodded as he absorbed her words—he didn't look shocked, or pitying or anything like that. Which she appreciated. Her childhood at times had been difficult, but it could have been a lot worse.

'You were looking for attention,' he said, and now it was Ruby's turn to be surprised.

'Yeah,' she said. 'I figured that out, eventually.'

Although that really was too simplistic. It had been more than that.

She'd wanted to be wanted. To be needed. Even if it was painfully temporary.

'Don't look so surprised,' he said. 'I'm no expert in psycho-analysis or whatever—I can just relate. It's why I started to act. My family is overflowing with academic over-achievers. But I hated school—hated sitting still. But acting…acting I could do. It was the one thing I was actually pretty good at.'

He'd grown up to be a lot more than a pretty good actor.

'Your family must be really proud of you.'

The little pang of jealousy she felt, imagining Dev's proud family, was unexpected. That was a very old dream—one based on stability, and comfort and permanence. She'd dreamt up castles in the sky, with her own prince and toothpaste-advertise-ment-perfect family. But she'd traded it in long ago: for a life that was dynamic, exciting and unencumbered. *Free.*

'Not particularly,' he said, his tone perfectly flat.

His words jolted her out of the little fairy tale she'd been imagining.

'Your family isn't proud of their world-famous son? I find that hard to believe.'

He shrugged. 'I don't know. Maybe they are. I don't have that much to do with them.'

She was going to ask more, but he suddenly pushed his chair back, scraping it on the wooden floorboards.

'You ready to go?'

He didn't bother waiting for her to reply; he'd already stood up.

'I thought we'd agreed to leave separately?' she asked. All in aid of not being photographed together.

Dev shoved a hand through his hair, then, without a word, walked out of the dining room.

Ruby didn't have enough time to wonder if he'd just left, kind of balancing out being, well, *nice,* for the past few hours—when he returned.

'The staff assure me there's been no sign of paparazzi, so I reckon we can risk it.'

She nodded. Really, there was no reason to leave together at all. But still—they did.

As they left she was hyperaware of him walking closely be-hind her—down the stairs, then to a private exit that avoided the busy main restaurant. His proximity made her skin prickle, but in the nicest possible way.

It was probably the wine, but she felt a little fuzzy-headed as she shrugged on her coat, so she was careful not to look at him. All of a sudden the reasons why she'd refused the date felt just out of reach.

He held the door open for her, and he caught her gaze as she stepped outside.

Something of her thoughts must have been evident in her expression.

'What are you thinking?' he asked.

They'd taken a few steps down the near-deserted back street before she replied. 'You confuse me,' she said. 'I had you pegged as an arrogant bastard, but tonight you've—*almost*—been nice.'

The warmth of his hand on her froze her mid-stride. He turned to face her, his fingers brushing down the outside of her arm, touching skin when the three-quarter sleeves ended. His fingers tangled with hers, tugging her a half-step forward.

She had to look up to meet his gaze. They were between streetlights, so his face was a combination of shadows, the dark-est beneath his eyes.

'No, Ruby,' he said. Quiet but firm. 'I think you had it right the other day, in my trailer.'

She racked her brain, trying to remember what she'd said—her forgetfulness a combination of being so red-hot angry at the time she'd barely known what she'd been saying, but more so just being so, so close to Dev. It was a miracle she could think at all.

'I'm not a very nice person.'

Then he'd dropped her hand, and was somehow instantly three steps away.

Her instinct was to disagree, to reassure him with meaning-less words. But she couldn't, because he wasn't talking about blackmailing her for a date, or being deliberately late to dinner—he wasn't talking about her at all.

And because she didn't understand, and because in that moment there was something in him she recognised, she didn't say a word.

Instead she moved to his side, and together, silently, they started walking.

CHAPTER SIX

DEV WASN'T REALLY thinking about where they were going. He just needed to walk.

But soon the rapidly increasing light and numbers of people that surrounded them heralded the direction he'd taken—and he looked up to the many, many steps that led to the opera house. He came to a stop, and took a deep breath.

He didn't know what to make of what had just happened.

Mostly, he would've preferred it hadn't.

Tonight—and this thing with Ruby—wasn't supposed to be about any of that.

'So,' he said, sounding absolutely normal. He *was* a good actor. 'Where to now?'

This area was well lit, a flat, paved expanse between the string of restaurants edging the quay and the massive sails of the opera house. Even though it was late, it *was* Sydney on a Saturday night, so there were many people around: most near the water, although some sat in pairs or strings on the steps. But right now, where they stood, they were alone.

She lifted her chin and smiled brightly—but unconvincingly.

She really wasn't a very good actor.

'How about we just wander for a bit?'

'Perfect,' he said—and it was. He'd half expected sparky, fiery Ruby to reappear, to announce that their date was over, their deal was done, and to disappear into the distance.

At the back of his mind he was bothered that he was so relieved, but, as he'd been doing so often lately, he filed that thought away. For later—and there was always a later.

In unspoken agreement they walked slowly towards the city—the wrought-iron railing that edged the quay to their right, and a line of old-fashioned sphere-topped lamp posts to their left. The breeze was cool off the water, but he welcomed its touch, his body over-warm beneath his open-collar shirt and suit jacket.

Ruby was talking, about *The Land,* about a play she'd seen at the opera house one time, about the rumours of some action-blockbuster sequel being possibly filmed in Sydney next year, and how she hoped to work on it. At first she seemed comfortable with his contribution of nods and murmurs, but eventually she started to draw him into the conversation. Asking questions about Friday's premiere, about whether it was really as bad as the papers had written today—that kind of thing.

'It wasn't my type of film,' Dev said. 'Maybe it was brilliant, just not for me.'

'So you thought it was boring?' she asked. He glanced at her, noting the sparkle in her eyes.

'Pretty much.'

She laughed. 'So weepy family sagas aren't for you.'

'No. I'm more an action/thriller kind of guy.'

'What a surprise,' she said, teasing him. 'Although, I had been wondering about that. Why *The Land?* Did you want a change of direction?'

'No,' he said, automatically, and harshly enough that Ruby slowed her pace a little, and looked at him curiously. 'I mean,' he tried again, 'yes, that was it exactly.'

'You don't sound all that sure.'

He wasn't. Right now he should be shooting a role he'd jumped at the opportunity to play. A negotiator in a smart, fast-paced hostage drama, a twist on the action-hero-type roles he was known for. But instead the role had been urgently recast, and his contract for his next film, with the now-burnt producer, had been torn to pieces. So here he was.

Only his previously stellar work ethic had prevented the story gaining traction. For now, the people involved had been relatively discreet, and Veronica had so far been able to mostly extinguish the—accurate—rumours.

But Ruby must have heard them—at least a hint of the truth. She watched him with curiosity in her gaze, but not the steeliness of someone determined to ferret out all the dirty details. She'd had all night to ask those questions—to push—but she hadn't.

He appreciated that.

'My agent had to twist my arm,' he said. That was the truth, at least.

He'd agreed only because he couldn't face another sleepless, pointless night in Hollywood. But he'd only traded it in for more of the same in north-west New South Wales.

Ruby was the only difference.

'You live in Sydney, right?' he asked, changing the subject.

They were walking amongst many people now—couples on dates, families, tourists with massive camera bags. If anyone recognised him, he hadn't noticed.

'Not any more,' she said.

'Melbourne?'

She shook her head. 'Not there either.' There was a smile in her voice.

Before tonight he hadn't been all that interested in getting to know the woman beside him. His interest in her had not been based around shared interests and the potential for meaningful conversation.

But at dinner, he'd found himself asking about *her,* and unsurprisingly that had led to him talking about elements of *himself* that he didn't share with his dates.

Maybe he was just rusty—it had been months since he'd gone out with a woman. Normally he had charming deflections of personal questions down to an art. He certainly didn't make a habit of welcoming them.

'If I name every city in the world until you say yes, we could be here a while.'

'And then you still wouldn't have an answer.'

They'd reached the end of the walk, and stood between the train station and ferry terminal.

Ruby was looking up at him, grinning—and waiting for him to do something with that non-response.

But he just left her waiting as he looked at her. Leisurely exploring the shape of her eyes, her nose, her lips. Beneath the CBD lights, he could see flecks of green and gold in her eyes he hadn't noticed before.

'You're beautiful,' he said, very softly, realising it was true.

Ruby took a rapid step backwards, and wobbled a little on her heels. He reached out automatically, wrapping his fingers around her upper arms to steady her.

For a moment her expression was soft. Inviting...

But then it hardened, and she shook his hands away.

'Nice try.'

'It's the truth,' he said, but immediately realised he was doing this all wrong as she glared at him. He didn't know how to handle this, why a compliment had caused this reaction.

'Look, it's getting late. Thanks for the lovely dinner. I'm going to head back to my hotel.'

She said all that, but didn't actually make a move to leave. If she had, he would've let her go, but that pause—he decided—was telling.

'If not Sydney, or Melbourne, or any other city in the world—where *do* you live?'

Ruby blinked as he deftly rewound their conversation. He could see her thinking, could see all sorts of things taking place behind those eyes.

'Wherever I feel like,' she said, slowly and eventually. 'I might stay where I've been working for a while. Or fly to stay with a friend for a few weeks. Or maybe just pick somewhere new I haven't been before, and live there.'

'But where's your base? Where you keep all your stuff?'

She shrugged. 'What stuff?'

'You don't own anything?'

'Nothing I can't keep in a suitcase.'

He took a moment to process this. 'Why?'

She smiled. 'I get asked that a lot. But the way I look at it, it makes sense. I've lived in some amazing places, seen incredible things. I'm not tied down—when I get a call offering me a job I can be on set, almost anywhere in the world, basically the very next day.'

'But don't you want a house one day?'

She wrinkled her nose. 'What? The great Australian dream of a quarter-acre block with a back pergola and a barbecue?' She shook her head. 'No, thanks.'

She spoke with the confidence of someone absolutely sure of their decision. He admired that—her assuredness. But he found it near impossible to believe. Could you really live your life the way she described?

'Most women your age are thinking marriage and babies. Putting roots down.'

'You're older than me,' she pointed out. 'Are you putting down roots? Is that what you're doing at your place in Beverly Hills?'

'Absolutely not,' he said. That was the last thing he wanted.

'Well, there you go.'

He must have looked confused, as she then tried to further explain.

'Is it so hard to believe? I told you before I'm a foster child, so my only "family" are the various sets of foster carers I called Aunty and Uncle. Nice people—great people—but, trust me, they couldn't wait to see the back of me, and I don't blame them. And nearly all my friends work in film, or did work in film, so they are scattered all over the place.'

He assumed he still looked less than convinced, as she rolled her eyes as if completely exasperated with him.

'No,' he said, before she tried again. 'I do get it.'

Didn't he, after all, live his life in kind of the same way?

Yes, he owned his home, but that was a financial decision, not one based on long-term planning—it wasn't a life goal or anything. He hadn't extrapolated that purchase into plans for the future: a wife, kids. Anything like that. In fact, he'd only ever had one goal: to act.

And now he wasn't even sure he had that.

'Do you want to get a drink somewhere?' he asked.

Ruby let the invitation bounce about in her brain for a moment.

'I should go,' she said. 'Like I said before. It's late, I—'

'But you didn't go.'

I know. She wasn't sure why. It had been the right thing to do—the right time to go. When he'd called her beautiful, she'd been momentarily lost. Lost in the moment and the pull of his warmth, and the appreciation she'd seen in his gaze. So, so tempting...

But then she'd remembered where she was—*who* he was—and why this was all a very, very bad idea.

'I should go,' she repeated. She'd meant to be more firm this time, but she wasn't—not at all.

'Probably,' he agreed. 'Based on what you've told me before—you should.'

He'd moved a little closer. *God.* He was good. He knew what he did to her when he was close. She could see it in everything he did—that arrogance, that confidence.

But unexpectedly, right now, it wasn't pushing her away.

Maybe because tonight she'd seen that confidence contrasted with moments of...not quite vulnerability, but *exposure.* He'd been raw, as if she was seeing Dev Cooper the man, not the actor.

And she'd found herself interested in that man. Oh, she'd always been *attracted* to Dev, by his looks, his charisma, by the persona his career had created. But that type of attraction was—with difficulty—possible to push aside. To be logical about. To walk away from, with the strict rules she lived by providing the impetus.

But *this* Dev. This Dev she couldn't so easily define. This Dev she wanted to know.

This Dev she wanted to understand.

No, thank you. But thank you for dinner...

It was suddenly impossible to say anything. She couldn't agree, but there was no other option.

So she was a coward and did nothing at all. But her expression must have portrayed her acquiescence, as he smiled—then grabbed her hand and tugged her after him.

They left Circular Quay, then headed a short way up Macquarie Street.

'Where are we going?' Ruby asked, belatedly.

He came to a stop. 'We're here,' he said. 'My hotel.'

They stood beneath a curved red awning—on red carpet, no less. A suited doorman stood only metres away, but when she glanced at him, he was carefully paying them no attention.

'This isn't cool, Dev, you said—'

'There's a bar on the ground floor, and the staff will guarantee we won't be disturbed—and certainly that no photos will be taken.' His lips quirked upwards—wickedly. 'I'm not inviting you to share a bottle of champagne as we roll about on my bed, Ruby.'

She knew she'd gone as red as the carpet. 'Oh,' she said. 'Of course not.'

'Shall we?' he said, gesturing at the brass-handled doors.

She nodded, and soon they'd made their way through the marble-floored foyer with its sumptuous oriental carpets to the hotel bar—a classic, traditional space. Full of heavy, antique wooden furniture, stunning silk wallpaper and chandeliers dangling with crystals, it was softly lit. A handful of people perched on bar stools, and a couple shared a drink at one table. Along one wall stretched a bench seat, upholstered in delicately patterned black and cream fabric. After Dev asked what she'd like to drink, she made a beeline in that direction, sinking gratefully into the soft cushioning, right in the corner of the room.

She watched Dev as he walked across the bar with their

drinks. He wore a dark suit, but no tie, and a crisp white shirt that was slightly unbuttoned. Somehow he made his outfit look casual and effortless, not formal at all. As if he'd happily wear the same outfit to do his grocery shopping, without a trace of self-consciousness.

The bar definitely was lit for mood, Ruby decided, but even so she was struck again by his unexpected gauntness. He didn't look unwell—just lean. But then, he'd eaten every bite of food in every course tonight...maybe he *had* been sick just like that rumour said? And now he was still putting weight back on. Or something.

She considered asking him, then immediately dismissed the possibility. Whatever had happened outside the restaurant—that moment—told her whatever was going on with Dev, whatever his private pain was, he would not discuss it tonight.

Besides—why would he? She was some random woman he'd even more randomly invited out for dinner.

She would never ask him those questions. They had this one night only.

He sat down, right next to her on the bench seat, rather than across the other side of the table as she'd expected.

Really? No. She hadn't honestly believed he'd do that. Of course he sat next to her, not quite touching—but touching was a very, very near thing.

He handed Ruby her wine glass, catching her gaze as he did so.

It was rather dark in this corner of the bar, she realised. Dark and...private.

His fingers brushed against hers and she jumped a little, making her wine splash about in its glass.

'Whoops!' she said, all nervous and breathy, and placed her glass firmly on the table, as if to somehow stabilise her thoughts.

The action was totally ineffective. She took a deep breath, but when she looked up—back into Dev's eyes—her mind went blank.

About all she was capable of at this moment, it appeared, was looking at Dev. And it *was* at Dev she was looking—not

Dev the movie star, but the Dev she'd just had dinner with. This Dev was an enigma—and this Dev, she liked.

He leapt from light to dark, revealing depth—maybe even pain?—that she never would have expected. And then he could slide so easily from teasing to darkly, insistently seductive.

As he was right now. Had he moved closer?

Maybe she had.

He knew she didn't want this, but in this way, at least, he was no gentleman.

He said he wasn't a nice person. Was this what he meant? This determined pursuit of a woman—of her—of what he wanted?

No, she decided. Not entirely. There'd been more, much more…

Ruby was losing herself in his eyes, his gorgeous, piercing blue eyes—but dragging her gaze away proved pointless, as she found herself staring at his lips.

It seemed the most natural, obvious thing in the world to lick her own lips in response.

Okay—now he *had* moved. When had he laid his arm across the back of the bench? She hadn't noticed at the time, but now it seemed a genius move, as it was so easy for his fingers to skim along the delicate, shivery skin of her neck.

Then up, up to her nape, his strong fingers threading through her hair, cupping her skull. But he didn't pull her towards him. Instead, he held her steady—but it really wasn't necessary.

As if she were going to duck her head, or look away now?

Then he was closer again, close enough that even in the dim light she could just see the red that was still in his eyes. For a moment she wondered what was wrong, felt a flash of concern for him…

But then that moment was gone, because she'd let her own eyes flutter shut, and all she could concentrate on was the feel of him breathing against her lips. So close, so close…

And then, finally, he kissed her.

For a crazy, silly moment her mind filled with images of Devlin Cooper kissing other women in movies. Of famous, romantic clinches, and of sexy, twisted sheets and picture-perfect lighting.

But then all that evaporated—as it was all make-believe. All utter Hollywood fantasy. This—this kiss—was real.

She was kissing a very real man. A man who had just teased her lower lip with his tongue. She leant into him, wanting more, needing more.

She needed to touch him, and she reached out blindly, her hand landing somewhere on his chest, then creeping up to his shoulders. His other hand was suddenly touching her, too, beginning at her waist, then creeping around to her back, beneath the little jacket she still wore. His hand splayed across her skin, not that she needed any encouragement to move closer.

He tasted like the wine they'd been sharing, like that crisp sorbet. Fresh. Delectable.

His kisses started off practised, but as she kissed him back, letting herself kiss him in the way he was making her feel, his kisses changed. They were less controlled, more desperate.

Ruby leant into him, matching him kiss for kiss, revelling in the feel and taste of his gorgeous, sexy, sinful mouth.

She felt incredible: beautiful, wanted.

She could sit here for ever, kiss him for ever…

But then his lips were away from her mouth, and trailing kisses along her jaw, up to her ear.

His breath was hot against her skin. So hot.

'Should we go to my room?'

Was that where this night had always been headed? Where they'd been headed since that dusty afternoon they'd first met?

Possibly? Definitely? Ruby didn't know—didn't care.

She just knew that standing now—on legs that would wobble—and leaving this bar for his room was the only imaginable option.

And so when he stood, and held out his hand for her, with that question still shining in his eyes, she knew what she was going to—what she had to—say.

'Yes.'

CHAPTER SEVEN

DEV LAY FLAT on his back on the sofa, staring up, in the dark, at the ceiling.

He was restless. Completely exhausted, but unable to sleep.

He'd tried pacing the considerable length of the penthouse's living areas, but it hadn't helped—from his experience pacing never did.

If anything his brain's wheels and cogs took the opportunity to whir ever faster, cramming his brain with all sorts of thoughts and ideas—leaving nowhere near enough room for sleep to descend.

He rubbed at his forehead, the action near violent. But as if he could simply erase all this crap away.

And it was crap. Useless, pointless, far-too-late-to-do-anything-about crap.

And so *random.* The stuff his subconscious was coming up with, that was building and festering inside him.

Snatches of time from his childhood.

Rare moments alone with his father.

Rarer words of praise—praise well and truly cancelled out with years and years of frustration and disappointment. At his failures—the straight As he never received, the sports he never mastered, the good behaviour he could never maintain.

And then memories of his brothers, so different from him, and yet who he'd admired so hard it hurt. Almost as much as he'd idolised his father—once.

Okay. Maybe not so random.

Of course he knew what this was about, it was as obvious as the watches his father had worn, the ones that had cost more than the average person's yearly wage, and that his father had made sure everyone noticed. But then, who could blame him? He'd worked *damn hard* for his money…

I worked damn hard, Devlin, and not so you could throw it all away. You know nothing about sacrifices—about what I would do for my family. Nothing.

He heard something—footsteps. Soft on the deep carpet.

He turned his head, and watched Ruby as she crept past. He couldn't see much in the almost pitch blackness, but she was most definitely creeping—her shoes dangling from one hand, each step slow and deliberate.

'Ruby,' he whispered. Then watched as she just about jumped out of her skin.

'Dev!'

He sat up and switched on a lamp, making Ruby blink at him in the sudden light.

She stood stock still, in her fancy dress and jacket—although her hair and make-up were somewhat worse for wear.

The reason for her déshabillé made him smile.

Although when he'd left his bedroom she'd been wearing only a sheet and a half-smile as she'd slept. *That,* he thought, was probably his favourite look for the evening. Or morning? Lord. Who knew what time it was any more?

'I thought you were asleep,' she said.

'Otherwise you would've said goodbye?' His voice was unexpectedly rough, rather than teasing as he'd intended.

'Yes—' she said. Then, the words getting increasingly faster, 'Actually, no. I mean, of course I would've said goodbye if you were awake, but I figured it was better if you were asleep. I didn't particularly want an audience for my walk of shame.'

His mouth quirked at her honesty. 'Shame, huh?'

She went pink. 'It's a turn of phrase. Of course I'm not ashamed. Just…' Her gaze flicked to the ceiling. 'This wasn't how I'd planned for the night to end.'

He didn't say 'me, either', because that wouldn't have been true.

It was just other elements of the night that had been unexpected, the moments where he'd looked at Ruby and felt…

He scratched absently at his bare chest.

He had no idea what he felt.

Her eyebrows rose, seemingly reading his mind. 'You are, at the very least, consistent in your arrogance.'

But there was a smile in her voice.

He shrugged unapologetically. 'I was right.'

She sighed, then readjusted the small gold handbag she had hooked over her shoulder. 'I should go.'

He nodded.

Dev went to stand, deciding he should at least be *chivalrous* enough to walk her to the door.

Maybe it was exhaustion. Maybe it was the way his legs had been bent on the too-short sofa, his left leg still weak from his accident—but either way, the result was that rather than ending up vertical, instead, he staggered.

Somehow Ruby was beside him, her arm wrapped tightly around his waist, just above the low-slung waistband of his boxer shorts.

'Careful!' she said, on a gasp.

Not that her slight weight would've made any difference if he'd been about to fall—which he wasn't. He'd tripped over his own feet—he was clumsy. That was all.

He went to shrug her off, annoyed at himself, and annoyed she'd thought he'd needed help.

'I'm fine,' he said. Short and sharp.

But she didn't let go, not completely. Her grip had loosened, but now her other hand traced over his skin, dipping into the slight hollows above and below his left hip.

'I didn't really notice before,' she said, very softly. 'It was dark and we were so caught up in the moment I didn't have much of a chance to look…'

Her fingertips trailed shivery trails across his belly, then up to the corrugation of his abdominal muscles—more defined than ever before. His trainer would be proud.

He meant to push her hand away, but didn't.

She looked up, straight into his eyes, and he was sure—absolutely positive—she was going to ask him what was wrong.

But at the last minute she didn't, and instead glanced away. Of all things, there was a grand piano in the corner of the room, and her attention appeared focused on its glossy black surface.

'I had a tummy bug a few weeks back,' he said, for some stupid reason feeling the need to provide an explanation. 'Lost some weight, and it's taking a while to put back on.' He shrugged. 'I have a fast metabolism.'

She looked up at him, and nodded, but didn't hold his gaze.

Her hand was still exploring, and she'd shifted slightly, so the arm around his waist was now more an embrace as she stood directly in front of him. Her fingers crept up one side of his body, tracing his pectoral muscle, over his flat nipple, then inwards to his breastbone. Then up, up, to the hollow at the base of his throat, across his collarbone, then curling, curling around to his neck.

But now her touch wasn't so gentle. She slid her fingers along his jaw, tilting his head back to her. His gaze connected with hers, darkest brown and startlingly direct.

'Is that why you can't sleep tonight?' she said, her words laced with scepticism.

'That's really none of your business.'

She closed her eyes for a long moment, then shook her head a little. 'No, of course not.'

He felt her begin to withdraw from him, her heat moving away.

His arms, that up to now hadn't moved from his sides, were suddenly around her, tugging her against him.

Her gaze fluttered up, her eyes widening. 'Dev?'

He didn't bother to explain—didn't even know how he would.

All he knew was that he wasn't ready for her to go yet.

So he leant towards her, and covered her lips with a kiss to silence her questions.

A crack between the heavy brocade curtains allowed the smallest slither of early morning light into Dev's bedroom.

Ruby lay on her side, her head propped up on one arm, staring at Dev's back as he slept facing away from her. Where the light hit his skin glowed a delicious olive: from the point of his shoulder it edged the side of his body, tapering gradually down from broad chest to narrow hips. There a sheet was bunched up, tangled around and over his legs.

He slept soundly, his breathing deep and regular.

Given their conversation of a few hours ago, she'd tried to wake him—to say goodbye. But he'd barely stirred when she'd gently touched—and later pushed—his shoulder, so she'd given up. Besides, given the shadows beneath his eyes that Hair and Make-up were spending so much effort covering up, he needed his sleep.

But she'd found getting out of his bed more difficult than she'd expected.

Before, when she'd woken alone, it had been easy. She'd basically leapt out of bed as her eyes had opened in the unfamiliar room—and reality had smacked her, hard.

What had she done?

No longer did a gaze she'd practically fallen into, or a touch that had made her whole body zap and tingle with electricity—let alone a kiss that was nothing like anything she'd ever experienced—cloud her judgment.

Now she could see the night for what it was. Not romantic, and surprising, and unexpected.

But a mistake.

Escaping had been the only option. Shoving the whole night somewhere right, right at the back of her mind where *one* day she might look back fondly and remember her date with a movie star.

Ha! More likely she'd remember what an idiot she was for falling for it.

Hadn't she gone beyond this? Beyond being impressed by looks, and a smile, and strength? Beyond decisions that were based on daydreams and chemical attraction—not sense and logic?

Apparently not—as she hadn't moved.

Dev moved though, and rolled onto his back.

In a flash Ruby was out of the bed, backing away until her heels hit the carpeted half-dozen steps that led to the penthouse's sunken bedroom.

But Dev slept on.

As she watched his chest rise up and down, Ruby felt like a complete idiot. So she didn't want him to wake up to see her still here but she *also* didn't want to leave?

She ran both hands through her hair in despair.

This was typical—there was *something* about Dev that had her thinking and acting in contradictions.

Maybe that something *is how he looked at me last night? The way he kissed me?*

Ugh! No, she wasn't going to do this to herself.

She was pretty sure she knew what she was doing—she was superimposing the heroes Dev had portrayed in his movies onto the man himself. Giving him traits that his characters—but not Dev—possessed. *Considerate, kind...or even brave, and mysterious...*

Naked, his leanness was blatantly obvious—with every breath each rib was brought into sharp relief. But maybe it was just what he said? A brief illness?

But none of the rumours rang true to Ruby. She didn't believe that he'd been sick, and if he pined for his supermodel ex, he was hiding it remarkably well. And party drugs? It just didn't fit.

She was sure there was something more—something darker. That there were layers to Devlin Cooper.

Or—maybe she should look at this more objectively.

He'd pursued her relentlessly, had arrogantly assumed he'd

get her into bed on the first night—and then promptly had, by being the perfect, charming date. In order to get just what he'd wanted, he'd become her ideal leading man.

He'd done what he was good at—act.

Yes. That was what had happened.

Here was no tortured soul—but simply an arrogant movie star.

So, silently, Ruby dressed, and, again in bare feet, made her escape.

She appreciated the lady at the concierge desk who raised not an eyebrow at her attire, and called her a taxi. Minutes later she was at her hotel, lying flat on her unslept-on bed.

She expected to be full of regret. She certainly should be.

She expected to be berating herself. Furious with herself.

And, she was—that was exactly what her brain was repeating in her head: that she'd made a mistake, that she'd been an idiot, what had she been thinking?

But instead all she could *feel* were memories of that moment she'd stared up into his eyes after he'd nearly fallen. Or out in the street outside the restaurant. Or the way he'd looked at her just before he'd kissed her in the bar.

Pain, passion. And lust, yes…but it had still been…special. In her heart—no matter what her brain was saying—she believed that she was different, that last night was special.

'And how stupid is that?' she said, aloud, and headed for a long, hot, shower.

CHAPTER EIGHT

WITH A LESS THAN elegant—but effective—movement, Ruby slammed the car door closed with her hip. She considered attempting to push the lock button on her key ring, but after thinking about how she would do that without putting down the pile of papers in her arms—and potentially seeing them fly off over the horizon in the stiff breeze—she decided her hire car was safe enough in a paddock in the middle of nowhere.

In her arms she balanced a reprint of this afternoon's sides, in blue to indicate they were the corrected versions. Today they were filming at the old farmhouse, a couple of kilometres from Unit Base. Really a farming family's actual home, they'd had to repaint the exterior to a less modern hue, and redecorate a handful of rooms—all of which would be returned back to their exact original state once filming was over. So, when she jogged up the wooden steps and through the propped-open front door, she walked into a home without a trace of the twenty-first century—at least not the parts that the cameras would see.

It was an aspect of filming Ruby had always enjoyed—this game of smoke and mirrors. When watching a finished film it never failed to amaze her that it made no difference she knew a staircase led to nowhere, or that a two-hundred-year-old stone cottage had really been built inside a sound studio. In the world of the film it was all real—and so she believed it, too.

Inside she stepped carefully over thick cables that crisscrossed the floor, the bright lights providing welcome warmth after the chill of the breeze outside. She squeezed between the crowds of crew until she found the on-set production assistant, who took the sides gratefully, and quickly filled Ruby in on the latest on-set dramas.

Of course Dev was there; she knew exactly which actors were filming today, so it wasn't a surprise to see him.

She'd been ready to see him this morning. To meet him at his car as had become customary. She'd practised talking him through his day, her standard nothing statements about being available to help him with anything—et cetera, et cetera. She'd been prepared, and totally fine about it—or at least had told herself that—but then she'd arrived at his car and he hadn't been there. And not in his trailer, either.

Graeme had been waiting, instead. To explain that Dev had arrived early, and would no longer require her assistance on set. Given his week of perfect punctuality—but mostly because *not* having to see Dev multiple times a day had massive appeal—she'd conceded.

So really, she should still be totally prepared to see him now. Yet, when she did—carefully only in her peripheral vision—she felt herself react, despite her best intentions. She wouldn't say her heart leapt—or anything so ridiculous—but there was definitely a lightness to her belly, and her skin went warm. She was unquestionably *aware* of him.

He sat at a rough-hewn kitchen table, his legs outstretched and his booted-feet crossed. He held a cardboard cup of coffee as he chatted to the director, that man's trademark baseball cap pulled down low.

If Dev was aware of her, there was absolutely no evidence of it. In his soft cream shirt, pushed up to his elbows and open at his throat, he looked the very epitome of relaxed. Not at all bothered that the woman he'd slept with not even forty-eight hours ago was five metres away.

Had he even noticed she was there?

Who cared if he did?

She was loitering—she'd done what she was here to do. She should leave.

So she did, circumventing the gaffer and the director of photography and their vigorous discussion about the room's lighting as she stepped out into the farmhouse hallway. The whole time—and it really bothered her she'd noticed this—Dev didn't as much as glance in her direction.

She made herself walk briskly to her car, as she really did need to get back to Unit Base, after all. She slid into her seat and slammed the door firmly behind her.

But instead of putting the key in the ignition, she found herself just sitting there for a moment, staring at the house.

What was she waiting for? For Dev to come charging out of the house, to wrench open the white hire-car door and pull her into his arms?

Certainly not. That was the last thing she wanted. No one could know what had happened between them. Ever.

It was good he'd ignored her. Perfect. Exactly what she wanted. She'd been relieved this morning when he'd cancelled her babysitting services—so what was different now?

Maybe because she was so much better at logical thought without Devlin Cooper in the vicinity.

She started the car, and drove carefully over a paddock rife with dips and potholes, her lips curving into a smile that was sadder than she would've liked.

Because really, this was laughable—that she cared that he'd so blatantly ignored her. That she'd created depth and layers and a *connection* with Devlin Cooper.

When of course, absolutely none of it—just like that early-nineteen-hundreds kitchen he'd been sitting in—had been real.

The unexpected creak of the cottage's front door opening had Ruby nearly leaping out of her chair. She glanced up at the loudly ticking clock on the production office wall: seven minutes past nine.

It was late. Very late. Even Paul had left twenty minutes ago.

It must be one of the security guards, checking up on her.

As she came to that logical conclusion she let out a breath she hadn't even realised she'd been holding, and smiled.

Who else would it be? The boogie monster?

'It's just me, Craig!' she called out to the slowly approaching footsteps. 'I'll just be a few more minutes.'

Her laptop made its little 'new email' pinging sound, and so her gaze was drawn in that direction as a man stepped into the doorway.

'Craig's having a beer with my driver, but I'll be sure to let him know.'

Ruby's gaze darted up—not that she needed the visual to confirm who that unmistakeable voice belonged to.

He'd propped himself up against the door's chipped architraving, as casual as you liked, in jeans and a black zip-up jumper.

For a moment her body reacted just as it had that afternoon in the farmhouse—every cell, every single part of her, suddenly on high alert. And for the same amount of time she was irrationally pleased to see him—long enough for her lips to form into the beginnings of a smile.

And then reality hit. The smile dropped, and Ruby stood up—abruptly enough that her chair skittered backwards on the floorboards.

'What are you doing here?'

He raised an eyebrow. 'Visiting you.'

'Why?'

Dev crossed his arms. 'Because I wanted to.'

Ruby realised she was wringing her hands and so pressed her palms down hard against the outside of her thighs. 'But today—' she began, then cut her words off as she realised where she was going.

He shrugged. 'I assumed the rules still applied—that you wanted no one on set to know.'

She shook her head. 'It doesn't matter. I mean, of course I don't want anyone to know, but I don't care that you ignored me. It was good, actually.'

Her words were all rambling and jumbled, and she sighed, resisting the urge to run her hands through her hair.

What was it about Dev?

Now Dev pushed away from the doorway. 'I wasn't ignoring you, Ruby,' he said, his voice low as he walked towards her. 'In fact, I don't think it would be possible for me to ignore you.'

He stood on the other side of her desk, watching her. He was so close, close enough that too many memories of Saturday night rushed right back to the surface, despite many hours of determinedly burying them all.

Most clear was the feel of his hands on her. Skimming across her skin, pressed against her back, gentle as they traced her curves.

She shivered, and that unwanted response snapped her back to the present.

'You should go,' she said. Very calmly.

He blinked, obviously surprised. 'Why?'

She laughed. 'Come on, we both know what Saturday was. You don't need to spell it out to me. I get it.'

'Get what?' he said, his forehead forming into furrows.

She sighed loudly. 'That it was a one-off.'

'You think I came here tonight to tell you that?'

'Why else would you be here?'

'I don't know,' he said, his gaze flicking to her lips. 'Maybe I was hoping for another kiss.'

It was so unexpected that Ruby was momentarily shocked silent. *Another kiss.*

It was…almost romantic. Somehow he'd taken what they had: a one-night stand—something you'd never associate with anything sweet or innocent, or meaningful—and ended up with that. A request for a kiss.

'That would be taking a couple of steps backwards, wouldn't it?' She spoke harshly, deliberately implying a tawdriness that the night they'd shared deserved.

He took a step back, as if she'd shoved him away with actions, and not only words.

His eyes were wide, and he went to speak—but then stopped.
His gaze sharpened. Darkened.

'Don't work too late,' he said.

Then turned on his heel, and left.

All week, his mum kept calling.

And every time, he let it ring out. She left messages, but after a while he didn't bother listening to those, either.

Couldn't listen, maybe?

It didn't matter.

He knew what she was calling about. The funeral. It had been more than three months now.

That first call, the worst one, hadn't been from his mum, but from his eldest brother, Jared. He was a doctor, a surgeon, actually, and he'd been using his doctor voice when Dev had answered his phone. As always, Dev had been on edge, used to his brother's patronising calls, his regular requests to visit home more often. That his mum missed him.

Never his dad.

But this call had been different. The doctor-voice had been the thinnest of veneers, and it had taken no time at all for Jared to crack. And that was when Dev had finally understood that something was very, very wrong.

A heart attack. No warning. Nothing that could be done.

Dad's dead. The funeral's next week. You can stay with Mum. It would be good for her, she's...lost.

Except he wasn't going to the funeral. And he didn't.

He was pathetic not to answer her calls, or to listen to her messages. Pathetic and weak and useless.

But he just couldn't do it—he just couldn't deal with it. Not yet.

It was ringing now, as it had every day since he'd arrived in Australia. Dev couldn't stand it, so he pushed away from his dining-room table to where his phone sat on the kitchen bench, and declined the call.

Gutless.

That was what he was.

Eventually he walked to his bedroom, around his bed and straight to the en suite. The tray of sleeping tablets was looking bare. He knew he shouldn't be taking them every night, his doctor had warned him of the dangers, of the side effects—but he couldn't risk what happened on his last film again. Back then, each night, he'd had every intention of making it to set the next morning. He'd had his alarm set well before his call, he'd re-read his script—everything. Then sleep wouldn't come at all, or he'd wait too late to take the tablet that would lead to oblivion. And by the time he woke up it was too late. Or—worse—he did wake up in time, but in the raw of the morning, before he'd had a chance to wake up, to remind himself who he was, how hard he'd worked, what he'd achieved…he honestly didn't care. He didn't care enough to get out of bed, to get to set. He didn't care about anything.

But this film was different. The mornings hadn't changed, not really—more often than not he slept through his alarm, or threw it across the room—but when Graeme knocked on the door he'd drag himself out of bed, and with every step he'd get a tighter grip of what he was doing, where he had to be, what he was doing that day.

He had his pride. He was a professional, and a damned good actor. A whole film crew was waiting for him.

Or at least it had been different. These last few days when Graeme had knocked, getting out of bed had been harder. He'd needed even more coffee once he'd hit Unit Base—enough that his own coffee machine had materialised in his trailer.

He swallowed the tablet, then cupped his hands under the running tap to collect enough water to wash it down. Water trickled down his neck, then down his bare chest, forming damp, dark spots along the waistband of his tracksuit pants.

He leant forward, staring into his eyes. Under the harsh lights, his eyes were red despite all the drops that Hair and Make-up were giving him. His face was a jumble of sharp angles and shadows, his skin dull…

This had to end.

He was over this. Over it, over it, over it, over it…

Tomorrow would be different.

He switched off the lights and flopped onto his bed, his skin too hot and his legs too restless to cover himself with even a sheet.

Tomorrow would be different.

If he kept saying it, one day it would actually be true.

Ruby hammered on Dev's front door. It was a really lovely door, with panels of stained glass, and part of her worried that she'd damage it. Only a very small part, though. A much bigger part of her wanted Dev to get his backside to Unit Base. Pronto.

'Don't worry,' said Graeme beside her. 'It won't break.'

He stepped forward with an air of much experience and put her hammering to shame, rattling the door with his heavy-fisted knocks.

The delicate glass held. The noise was deafening. But there was still no sign of Dev.

'Do you have a key?' she asked, trying to peer through the multicoloured glass.

'No,' he said.

Ruby took a step back and put her hands on her hips as she surveyed the house.

Paul had called her to his office barely thirty minutes ago, and she'd shot out of her office and to Dev's cottage in record time. Unfortunately, Dev's call had been ten minutes prior to Paul's *'Where the hell is Devlin Cooper?'* rant, and with every minute that passed—and with a twenty-minute drive back to Unit Base…

Basically she needed Dev out of his house and into his car *now*.

There were only two windows on the front of the sandstone cottage, edged in dark red brick. Both were closed, and a quick test proved they weren't going to open easily. The white-painted veranda wrapped around the side of the house, and Ruby followed it, stopping at each window to check for an entry point. So far—no luck.

The back of the house was a modern extension, with the veranda opening out into a deck with views to the mountains—not that Ruby paid any attention to it. Instead she zeroed into a flash of pale colour—curtains that were flapping through a small gap in the sliding doors. It was only a small gap—did that mean Dev hadn't closed it properly when he'd left? Or when he'd returned?

Ruby hoped like heck it was the latter, because he certainly wasn't on set—her phone had remained silent—so if he wasn't in the house she had no idea where on earth to look for him next.

She had to push the door open to create a space large enough to walk through. She stepped through the curtain, pausing a moment to untangle herself from the heavy fabric. Inside it was dark—gloomy despite the sunny day outside. And silent—completely silent.

For the first time it occurred to Ruby that maybe Dev hadn't simply slept in. She'd immediately assumed he was lounging about, deciding he had more important things to do than—you know—his job.

'Dev?' she called out. Or meant to. Instead she managed little more than a whisper.

She cleared her throat, and tried again. 'Dev?'

Again—silence. This shouldn't be surprising given the noise she and Graeme had been making was infinitely louder, and had certainly elicited no response.

But still, only now did Ruby worry.

What if the rumours were true?

She knew many celebrities kept their addictions well hidden—many more did not—but Dev... She just couldn't believe it. She'd spent a night with him—surely she would've guessed?

She stood in the lounge room, and it was clearly empty. The hallway beckoned, and she broke into a run, throwing open doors as she went.

Bedroom—empty.

Study—empty

What would she know, or could she know, really, about Dev?

She thought of his gaunt frame, the sometimes emptiness in his gaze. Not all the time, and certainly not when he'd been looking straight at her—but there'd been moments when there'd been depth and flickers of so much…

No. She needed to stop that, needed to stop imagining things that weren't there. Romanticising no more than a forgettable collection of moments in time.

And she would forget them, eventually.

Right now she needed to focus—on her job, why she was here. She needed to find Dev and get him on set.

Her phone trilled its message notification, but she didn't bother to check. She knew what it was—Paul. Wanting to know where she was, and why she wasn't on set with Dev already. Five minutes ago, even.

Another room—a larger space, a sitting room. Also empty.

The next—a bedroom.

Occupied.

The door creaked on old hinges as she flung it all the way open, and rattled a vase on a side table when it smacked against the wall.

Then she was at the bed, kneeling on the soft mattress as she reached across the wide expanse to grab onto a bare male shoulder. And shake it—hard.

'Dev! Wake up.'

A sheet was twisted around his legs, and his skin was covered in goose pimples in the freezing room, the air-conditioning unit on the wall bizarrely turned on high.

She shook him again. 'Damn it, Dev!'

Her heart raced, her breath caught in her throat.

Then all of a sudden he moved, rolling effortlessly onto his back, his eyes opening slowly.

Ruby let out her breath in a huge sigh of relief, dropping her hands onto her knees. For a minute or so she just took deep breaths, staring down at her own hands as they gripped her jeans.

'You scared me half to death,' she eventually managed.

He reached up, rubbing at his eyes, his movements deliberate and heavy. He turned his head on the pillow to look at her, his lips tipping up into a smile.

'Good morning,' he said, all husky and unbelievably sexy.

'Oh, no,' she said. 'It is *not* a good morning, Mr Cooper. You're late.'

He blinked, obviously confused. Rather than reply, he reached for her, his fingers grazing along the denim covering her thigh.

'Come here,' he said.

She scooted back, but probably not as fast as she should. He grabbed her hand before she slid off the bed, tugging her towards him with a strength she hadn't expected. Or maybe it was just that she didn't resist.

Somehow she was right up beside him, leaning over him, her legs pressed up against the bare skin of his waist, and his hip where his tracksuit bottoms had slid down just a little.

She looked down at him, at his incredibly handsome face— even in the gloom and with pillow creases on one cheek—and forgot what she'd been about to say.

He still held her hand, clasped on top of her legs, and a finger traced hypnotic patterns across the delicate bones beneath her knuckles.

His other hand reached across his body, to touch her other arm where it hung uselessly beside her—neither touching him nor pushing him away. His touch slid upwards, feather light, following the shape of her wrist, her forearm, her elbow, then jumping across, and around her, to her back. And then—he pulled her against him.

She gasped as she fell, landing across his chest. He was warm now, hot, in fact, and her body was fast catching up as his hands travelled across her back.

Ruby looked directly into his eyes, eyes that were anything

but empty. A gaze that she found compelled her, questioned her, wanted her.

So she leant towards him, towards all that, then closer, closer, their kiss mere millimetres, mere milliseconds away…

And then she was gone—off the bed and metres away, her back to him as she took deep, deep, what-the-hell-am-I-doing? breaths.

She shouldn't be doing this. No. She *couldn't*.

Then behind her, he laughed. A low, unexpected sound that reverberated all the way down to her toes.

She spun around, her nails digging into her palms as her hands formed into furious fists. 'What's so funny?'

He'd sat up, his shoulders propped against the wrought-iron bed head. His gaze flicked over her, from her long boots and jeans up to her layers of vests and thin wool jumpers to keep her warm in the cool spring air.

'You,' he said. 'This. What *is* your problem?'

'*My* problem?' Ruby said, and then swallowed, trying to re-locate her brain—and, while she was at it, any sense of profes-sionalism she still possessed. 'The only problem I have is that you were required on set—' she pulled her phone out of her pocket to check the time '—over an hour ago.'

For the shortest of moments his eyes flickered, and his ex-pression shifted. He looked—surprised? Disappointed? Angry?

Then it had all disappeared to be replaced by a look she was all too familiar with—arrogance.

He tilted his head back, so it rested against the wall. Then slowly and deliberately, he turned his head towards her, every pore of his body oozing exactly how little he cared.

It was all very…*practised.*

Ruby's eyes narrowed as she met his, trying to see past this hastily erected façade, trying to figure out…*Dev,* really.

No. She didn't have time for this.

'I need you to get a move on, Mr Cooper. So we don't lose the whole morning.'

He nodded. 'Yes,' he said. 'I can see how you would need that.'

Dev didn't move.

Ruby stepped forward, and Dev's gaze dipped to her still-fisted fingers. 'Exactly what do you think you're going to do with those?'

Instantly her fingers were flat against her thighs.

'Are you unwell, Mr Cooper?'

He shook his head. 'I think you're quite aware how healthy I am.'

Ruby's cheeks went hot, but she pushed on, now right beside the edge of the bed. 'Then I really need you to get out of bed immediately. A lot of people are waiting for you.'

He shrugged. Then he looked pointedly at her hands—again fisted. But this time she made no move to relax them. Much more of this and she might well *actually* hit him.

'Mr Cooper. I'm sure you're aware of your contractual ob-ligations.'

'Of course,' he said, with a nod. But then did not elaborate further.

Ruby swallowed a sigh. He knew the deal—this far into film-ing and with Arizona due to leave the country, there was *no way* that Paul could replace Dev. Besides, it wasn't as if there were a bevy of other A-list actors banging down the producer's door.

'Fine,' she said. 'Let's get to the point. I want you on set as soon as possible. You—for reasons unknown—have chosen to stay in bed today. And—inexplicably—despite the dozens of people relying on the success of this film, wish to stay here.'

'I'd agree with that assessment.' His voice was as dry as dust, his expression patently unmoved.

'So tell me,' she said, making absolutely no attempt to sound professional any more, 'what exactly do I need to do to get you out of this room?'

At this, he smiled. A real smile—a delicious smile. A smile that moved the heat still in her cheeks to somewhere low in her belly. It was a visceral reaction she couldn't have prevented if she tried.

And Ruby had the sudden realisation that this was where Dev had been heading the whole time. To this question.

'A favour,' he said.

He'd locked his gaze to hers. A gaze she didn't have a hope of interpreting.

Why did she even bother? Hadn't she decided he was just an actor, portraying whatever emotion or personality that would get what he wanted out of a situation?

'What type of favour exactly?'

Another shrug. 'I haven't decided yet.'

She gaped at him. 'You don't seriously expect me to agree to that?'

He didn't say a word, just looked at her. Then, after a while, slid down along the mattress until his head hit the pillow. Then, as calmly as you liked, turned onto his side. His back to her.

Ruby's mind raced, considering her options.

Could she go and find Graeme? Get him to somehow strong-arm Dev out to the car?

A quick glance at Dev, and his muscled physique and sheer size nixed that idea. No, that wouldn't work.

She could call Paul?

And...what? Her job was to solve problems. Paul expected her to solve things—once he gave her a problem, quite simply it ceased to be his. It was *her* problem.

'It can't be illegal,' she said, finally.

He casually turned over, to smile that devastating smile at her yet again, his chin propped on one hand.

My God. She was helpless to prevent the rapid acceleration of her heat—even at completely inappropriate moments, her body reacted to him.

'It won't be.'

'And it can't be a...' Ruby had to look away, staring at the elaborate cornicing above the curtains '...a kiss,' she said. Then faster, 'Or anything else like that.'

In seconds he was up, out of bed, standing right in front of her, forcing her to look at him. The emptiness had gone, but what he'd exposed was impossible to interpret.

'Is that how little you—?' he started. Then stopped.

Then in a different, heavier tone, the shutters firmly up again, he spoke. 'No.'

Ruby backed away, needing to put space between them.

'So you'll come now? Right this instant?'

He nodded.

'Okay,' she said. 'Fine. A favour. Done.'

She thought she'd get that smile again—but didn't. He just kept looking at her, revealing not a thing.

So she backed away even further, right outside the room and into the hallway.

'You've got two minutes to meet me out the front,' she said, briskly. Like Production Co-ordinator Ruby, not the Ruby who'd very nearly kissed Devlin Cooper again.

She didn't wait around for him to respond, she was just out of there. Away from him, away from the mass of confusion and attraction and questions and heat that was every encounter with Dev.

Outside, on the decking, she stared up at the cloudless sky. Just stared and stared and stared.

And wondered what on earth she'd just agreed to.

What on earth she'd just done.

CHAPTER NINE

DAYS PASSED. A week.

Nothing.

Ruby barely saw Dev at Unit Base, and the few times she did get out to set he didn't even notice she was there—or at least certainly gave the impression he didn't.

When she ate dinner at the pub a few times after work, she deliberately kept her back to the door and talked and laughed with her friends as normal—because it wasn't as if she cared if Dev arrived or anything.

And then she hated herself for looking over her shoulder whenever a footfall was somehow heavier or different or whatever. Just in case.

Occasionally she'd kid herself that he'd forgotten about their deal. That he was half asleep and didn't remember, or that he'd never meant it anyway.

But she didn't, truly, believe that.

So late on a Saturday afternoon, after a six-day work week and with every cell in her body desperate to crawl into bed and sleep straight through until Monday, it didn't really surprise her to see Dev sitting on the jarrah bench seat outside her apartment.

Equally, it didn't surprise her when her heart did a little somersault. Didn't surprise her—but she wasn't exactly happy about it either.

He wore jeans, T-shirt and a black jacket. A rugby team's baseball cap was pulled down low over his forehead, and dark sunglasses covered his eyes. He pushed himself to his feet as she slid out of her car.

Ruby locked the doors, and walked towards him as nonchalantly as possible, fumbling only slightly as she located her key.

'Is this your version of going incognito?' she asked as she stepped onto the small porch. 'As I don't think you're fooling anyone.'

'You'd be surprised how many people don't recognise me,' he drawled, catching her gaze with a pointed look.

For what felt like the hundredth time since they'd met, Ruby blushed, and she turned her head to give the task of opening the door her complete attention.

'You'd better come inside before the whole town starts talking,' she said as the door swung open. 'Apparently my motel manager tops even the local hairdresser in knowing all the Lucyville gossip.'

'That's a real issue for you, isn't it?' he asked, following her inside. 'People talking about you?'

Inside her apartment Ruby wasn't exactly sure what to do. After all, she had no idea why Dev was actually here.

'I would've thought you'd understand that,' she said, throwing her handbag onto the tiny kitchen bench. 'Given how much the world gossips about you.'

Tea, she decided. She'd make them both a cup of tea.

'For me, gossip's a necessary evil. I can't expect all the perks of fame without some of the crap.'

Ruby flicked the switch on the kettle, then found two coffee mugs that she placed onto the laminate counter. One had a chip on the handle.

Somehow, making tea for Dev in this simple little apartment seemed more surreal than anything else that had happened between them. She rubbed her thumb over the chip a few times, trying to pull her thoughts together.

Why was he here? What favour was he going to ask of her?

Dev was resting both his hands on the other side of the counter, watching her. 'Ruby?'

What were they talking about again?

'Gossip,' she said, reminding herself. 'Well. I'm not famous, obviously. So there's no real positive out of people spreading rumours about me, is there? Wouldn't it be more strange if it *didn't* bother me?'

'But you seem slightly more…obsessed with maintaining a lily-white reputation. Not one whisper of scandal is allowed when it comes to Ruby Bell. No hint of the slightest moment of unprofessionalism.'

Ruby snorted most inelegantly. 'My reputation is not lily white, I can assure you.'

Dev raised his eyebrows, but Ruby just shrugged as she flipped open a box of teabags and dropped one into each mug.

'I told you the other night that I had a bit of a wild youth. Well, unsurprisingly, that type of behaviour generates gossip. A lot of gossip. Some of it accurate, a lot of it not. According to the local grapevine, it's quite frightening the number of people I slept with as a seventeen-year-old.'

Ruby smiled as she reached for the boiled kettle and saw Dev's expression. 'Don't look so shocked. I wasn't as bad as people made out, but I did enough to deserve a good chunk of my reputation. I'm not proud of myself—but it's done now. I was very young, very naïve. But I've learnt, moved on—I'm not the same person any more.'

'You're not the type of person who gets gossiped about.'

Dunking the teabags, she looked up, pleased he'd understood. 'Yes, exactly. I had enough to deal with back then without the speculating glances, the whispers and the innuendo. In fact, gossip made my behaviour worse—I confused people talking about me with people actually giving a crap about me. Although, for a while, just being noticed was enough.' Ruby paused, and laughed without humour. 'And you know what? I was the one who figured out I needed to change, that I needed to grow up, and not one judgmental comment by some know-it-all busybody made one iota of difference.'

Too late she realised she'd raised her voice, and tea was now splashed in tiny droplets across the counter.

'Oh,' she said, in a small voice. Then stepped away, snatching up a tea towel and blotting ineffectually at the hot liquid.

Dev was now in the kitchen with her, and he reached out, taking the towel from her.

'What happened?' he asked.

She looked down at her feet, and wiggled her toes in her ballet flats.

'I didn't say anything happened,' she said.

'But it did.'

She looked up abruptly, her lips beginning to form the words and sentences to explain…

Then she realised she was standing in a two-and-a-half-star holiday apartment with peeling vinyl flooring with one of the most famous men in the world.

No, he really didn't need to know about any of what happened.

So she remained silent.

For a long minute she was sure he was going to push—but he didn't.

Instead he calmly picked up the coffee mugs and tipped their remaining contents down the sink.

'We don't really have any time for a drink, anyway,' he said, his back still to her.

'Why's that?' she replied, for a moment, confused. Then, in a flash, she remembered—the only possible reason why he was here. She swallowed. 'The favour.'

He turned slowly, then leant his hips against the cabinets. Belatedly, he nodded.

'Our plane leaves in just over an hour.'

Ruby knew her mouth was gaping open, but was helpless to do anything about it.

Dev smiled. A devilish smile that was becoming so, so familiar.

'We have a party to attend. In Sydney. No time to drive so I chartered a plane.'

As you did.

'A party?' Ruby asked, when her jaw had begun functioning again.

'It's just casual, at a private home. A birthday party of a— friend.'

He said it as if that was all the information she could possibly need. When she stood, just staring at him, his eyes narrowed impatiently.

'You really need to go pack.'

'What if I have plans tonight?' she asked.

He shrugged. 'You agreed to the deal.'

'I didn't agree to put my life on hold at your whim.'

He grinned. 'Lord, Ruby, I do like you.'

She shook her head, dismissing what he said. 'I have plans tonight.'

Plans involving instant noodles and a small pile of romantic comedy DVDs, but still—plans.

'Well, you should've thought of that at the time. Negotiated appropriate methods of notification of the favour or something—but, you didn't. So—here we are. And I'd like to cash in my favour. Tonight.'

Ruby considered continuing her argument. Or just flat out refusing to go. He wouldn't, after all, drag her out of her apartment against her will.

Maybe he saw what she was thinking in her eyes.

'It's just a party, Ruby. Nothing sinister, I promise. You might even have fun.'

But still, she hesitated. He was so brash, so sure of getting his way…

'I really don't want to go on my own.'

That sentence was said much more harshly than what had come before. But oddly, without the same self-assurance. Quite the opposite, in fact.

And so, somehow, she found herself packing her little red carry-on suitcase.

Then minutes later she was sitting beside him in the back seat of Dev's four-wheel drive, zipping along as Graeme drove them to the airport. And to the mysterious party beyond.

The luxurious Cessna took less than an hour to cover the four hundred and fifty kilometres between the single-runway Lucyville airport—the home of the local aero-club and certainly no commercial airlines or chartered jets—and the private terminal adjacent to Sydney International airport.

Unsurprisingly, Ruby had asked a lot of questions in the drive to the Lucyville airport. Dev had responded carefully with as few words as possible:

Whose party is it? *Ros.*

And she was? *A friend.* He'd managed to say this more confidently this time—regardless, Ruby had still raised an eyebrow.

How many people could be there? *Fifty?* He had no idea.

Where was it? *Her house.*

Why don't you want to go alone?

To this, he'd simply shrugged, and by then they'd arrived at the small strip of tarmac amongst the patchwork paddocks— and there was no more time for questions.

Take-off was taken up with a safety demonstration by their stewardess, plus a bit of oohing and aahing by Ruby over their plush leather seats that faced each other and the glossy cabinetry in the little food and beverage galley behind the cockpit.

'This is completely awesome,' she'd said at the time. Dev agreed—money made life a lot easier and, at times like this, a lot more fun.

Fortunately, in this instance, it also distracted Ruby from her quest to discover exactly where they were going.

During the short flight she was ensconced in the jet's tiny bathroom, courtesy of his explanation that they would need to drive direct from the airport to the party. This had earned him yet another glare, and then later another—from freshly made-up eyes—as she'd buckled up next to him for landing, plucking at the fabric of her jeans.

'I really didn't have anything suitable to wear.'

'You look fantastic,' he'd said—sincerely—running his gaze over her brown leather heeled boots, dark blue jeans, creamish camisole and navy blue velvet blazer.

She'd just rolled her eyes. Which—again—she'd repeated when he'd quickly changed on arrival in Sydney.

'Two minutes to look like *that*? Really?'

But she'd smiled, and he'd been stupidly pleased that she'd approved of how he looked.

Now they sat in the back seat of another black four-wheel drive, this time with a new driver, Graeme having been left a little flabbergasted back in Lucyville. But then, he couldn't do much given Dev hadn't booked him onto the flight.

Which hadn't been a difficult decision. No doubt he'd hear all about it from Veronica—sooner rather than later. But right now, it was all about tonight.

Ruby made a few attempts at conversation, but all fell flat. Instead Dev found himself staring at nothing out of the window, Sydney passing him by in a multicoloured blur of lights. As their destination became closer, even the lights failed to register as his eyes completely unfocused.

Then he didn't know what he was looking at, or thinking about. *Nothing* he told himself, but of course he wasn't.

Snatches of voices, bursts of laughter, moments of anger, conspiratorial giggles. Memories. None fully formed, more a collage, a show-reel of moments in time. All set in one place, at one house—at one home.

When the driver pulled into the familiar ornate gates, Dev waited for the crunch of flawlessly raked gravel—but there was none. The tyres rolled across a driveway that had been paved perfectly smooth some time in the past fourteen years.

The driver expertly negotiated the cars parked along the semi-circular curve, pulling to a stop directly before the tiered garden steps that led to the front door.

Ruby opened her own door, stepping out of the car almost the moment the car rolled to a stop. Hands on hips, she stood, surveying the house, the gardens—and the guests who flowed around them, walking up from the street in couples and groups.

Dev sent the driver on his way and joined Ruby, watching her watch what was happening around her.

Up until this moment she'd displayed not one hint of nervousness about the evening. Yes, she'd been a little bothered about the lack of time to prepare, and had sighed loudly at his halfway answers to her questions. That she was frustrated with *him,* there was no doubt.

But otherwise she'd been typically no-nonsense Ruby. Just as she was on set, she'd been calm, and focused. He'd almost been able to read her thoughts: *It's just a party. No big deal.*

Now they were here, however, he could see sudden tension in her posture.

She turned towards him, tiny lines etching her forehead.

'Who am I?' she asked.

It took him a moment to figure out what that meant.

'You mean if anyone asks?'

Her answering nod was terribly stiff.

Lord. He didn't know. He barely knew why *he* was here, let alone how he should describe his unexpected guest.

'My—'

He was going to say *date,* for the reward of that flash to her eyes—that delicious reaction of heat tinged with anger.

But tonight he found riling her was not on the top of his list of things to do.

So no—he wouldn't push, he wouldn't call this a date when he knew in her head she'd so stubbornly decreed that they would never, ever date again.

'—friend,' he finished.

It sounded lame—and like a lie. As much of a lie as calling *Ros* a friend.

And somehow it was also the wrong thing to say, as Ruby took a big step back, then looked away, staring up at the moon.

'How about we just go with work colleague?' she said, with a razor-sharp edge.

He didn't have a chance to respond, or to even begin to figure out what he'd done wrong, when she began to stride towards the house.

He caught up with her well before they reached the door, where a smartly dressed man—but still obviously a security guard—widened his eyes as he recognised him.

He opened the door for them without a word, and inside, in a redecorated but still familiar foyer, a small crowd of guests mingled.

Ruby looked at him curiously, and he knew what she was thinking. The guests were all older than them, by a good twenty or thirty years.

But then the enthusiastic chatter stilled, and one by one people turned to face him, replacing their cacophony with whispered speculation.

Then, from amongst it all, out stepped a women with silver-blonde hair styled in the sleekest of bobs, and an elegant dress that flattered a figure still fit and trim at—as of today—sixty.

Her eyes, so similar to his, were wide, and coated in a sheen he didn't want to think about too much.

As dignified as always, she approached them politely. Although her smile went well beyond that—it was broad. Thrilled.

Dev felt his own mouth form into a smile in response—not as wide, not as open, yet he still had the sense he'd been holding his breath for hours.

He reached for Ruby, wrapping his hand around hers in an instinctive movement.

'Ruby, this is Ros,' he said, 'my—'

'Mother,' she finished.

Ruby didn't look at him, she simply smoothly accepted the hand that his mum offered, and wished his mother a happy birthday.

'I'm Ruby,' she added, 'a colleague of Dev's.'

His mother glanced to their joined hands, then back to Dev, questions dancing in her eyes.

But no, he wasn't about to explain.

A long moment passed, and Dev realised he'd made a mistake. He should've hugged his mum, or something…but he'd felt frozen. Out of practice.

Then it was too late, and his mum said something that was terribly polite, and trilled her lovely, cultured laugh, and disappeared back into the crowd. A crowd now full of disapproving expressions, all aimed in his direction.

Yes, he knew who he was—the son who'd blown off his father's funeral.

This is a mistake.

He still held Ruby's hand, and he would've tugged her outside, straight back to their car, if more guests hadn't filled the space behind them. Instead, he pulled her into one of the front rooms—'the library', his mum called it, with its walls of multicoloured books and oriental carpets.

Or at least he thought he'd drawn Ruby into the room—belatedly he realised it was more Ruby doing the directing. Inside, she dropped his hand, and pushed the door shut behind them, hard enough that it verged towards a slam.

'This is your *mother's* birthday party, Dev?' she said. Then on a slightly higher pitch, 'You invited me to your *mother's* birthday party?'

He nodded, because there was nothing else he could do.

Her hands were back on her hips again, and she took a long, deep breath. 'Okay. So, do you want to hurry up about telling me *what on earth* is going on?'

Ruby was doing her absolute best to hold herself together. What she wanted to do—desperately—was throw something in Dev's direction. Something hard, preferably.

What the hell was he playing at? Just who did he think he was?

A floor lamp glowed in the corner, and flames flickered in

the fireplace, throwing soft light across the room and making the dark leather of the button-backed chesterfield lounge suite shine.

Into that shininess, Dev sank, stretching his legs out long before him. He tilted his head backwards, resting it along the back of the sofa, and stared upwards, as if the delicate ceiling rose suddenly required his full attention.

'We can go in a minute,' he said, just before she was about to speak again.

The low words—quiet and so unexpected—had her swallowing the outburst she'd had ready.

All of a sudden the fight went out of her—and all she could remember was the reason she'd agreed to come here in the first place: *I really don't want to go on my own.*

'Go?'

He looked at her. 'Yeah. There's a restaurant I like, at Darling Harbour. I won't have any trouble getting us in.'

Ruby had been standing near the door, but now she crossed the room, perching on the edge of the single chesterfield armchair directly across from Dev, her booted feet only inches from his distressed leather loafers.

'Why would you want to leave your mother's birthday party? I bet it's a milestone, too, given all these people.'

'Her sixtieth.'

Ruby nodded. 'So why leave?' she repeated.

He stood up abruptly, and shoved both hands into his pockets. 'It was a dumb idea to come. I don't know what I was thinking.'

'How was it a dumb idea to come to your own mother's birthday party?'

Dev's gaze was trained on the fire, and he stood perfectly still.

'It just was. Is.'

Now he looked at her, but in the uneven light she couldn't read a thing. 'I'm confused,' she said.

He shook his head dismissively. 'You don't need to understand. Let's go.'

His fingers wrapped around the door handle, but before he had a chance to twist it open Ruby was on her feet.

'I don't need to understand?' she asked, far from politely, stepping closer so they were almost toe to toe. 'You're telling me I'm supposed to just accept that you whisked me across the state *and* deliberately concealed our exact destination—and ask no questions?'

'Yes,' he said. 'That would be ideal.'

Dev rubbed his forehead, not looking at her. In the flickering shadows, the darkness beneath his eyes was suddenly even more pronounced.

Without thinking, Ruby reached out, running a finger whisper-soft along the top edge of his cheekbone.

At her touch, his hand dropped to his side, but otherwise he didn't move a muscle.

'Does tonight have something to do with *this?*' she asked, her fingertips tracing across to the smudges of black beneath his eyes.

For long moments, their gazes met, his momentarily open and revealing above her exploratory touch.

That his unspoken answer was *Yes,* was obvious—but there was more. A lot more.

His eyes revealed a depth of emotion she'd only seen before in glimpses. But now, right this second, he'd set it all free— for her to see.

But what was she seeing? Sadness, she knew. She recognised. And loss. Guilt?

But then it was all gone, gone as quickly as he gently but firmly took her wrist and pushed it away.

'Let's go,' he said. Again, he reached for the door.

Ruby touched him again, covering his much larger hand partially with hers.

'I think we should stay.'

He was staring at their hands. Ruby could feel the tension beneath her palm, the rigid shape of his knuckles.

'Why?'

'Because you want to stay.'

He looked up, his eyebrows raised. 'And how, exactly, do you know that?'

She had no idea. But she did.

She shrugged, deciding it best to say nothing at all. She stepped away, lifting her hand away from his, conscious that she really had no idea what was going on here. That she was the last person in the world who should be advising anyone on their own family issues.

Dev was right, really—there was no reason she needed to understand any of this. Not why Dev brought her here, not why he wanted to leave—and certainly not why Dev's beautiful mother would look at her son with such a mix of instantaneous joy and pain.

She shouldn't *want* to understand. There was no point.

She was no one to him. *A friend,* he'd said, for the evening. That wasn't even true, and yet still she'd felt a stupid, stupid kick to her guts when he'd said those words.

Work colleague was the accurate term. The only term to describe them.

She stepped away, suddenly terribly uncomfortable. As she knew all that, believed all that—and yet all she could think about was Dev, and those dark eyes, and that sorrow behind them.

'I think we should stay.'

Ruby's head jerked up at the deep, firmly spoken words. As she watched, Dev opened the door, holding it open for her.

He looked relaxed and utterly unbothered. As if he'd always been the one who'd wanted to stay the whole time, in fact.

He motioned towards the door. 'Ready?'

Ruby just nodded in response, and then he followed her out into the hallway.

The party spread from the three-storey home's expansive entertaining areas through concertinaed bi-fold doors to the garden. Tall stainless-steel patio heaters dotted the grass, and fairy lights wound their way through the ornamental hedges and carefully pruned gardenias. The thirty-metre high Ironbarks and Turpentines of the adjacent Sheldon Forest—imposing even at night—formed a towering backdrop to the evening.

It was—clearly—yet another fabulous party hosted by Ros Cooper.

For about the twentieth time in the two minutes since he'd walked out of the library, Dev changed his mind.

He'd been right. He should go.

'Devlin!'

Dev bit back a groan, but turned to face that familiar voice.

'Jared!' he said, as forced and false as his eldest brother.

He blinked as his gaze took him in. How long had it been? Two years? Five?

Jared had softened just a little around the middle, and his temples sported new sprinklings of grey. But his expression—anger mixed with frustration mixed with judgmental dismissal—that was remarkably unchanged.

Actually, not remarkable at all. Jared, like his father, wasn't known for his swift changes of opinion.

It took barely a minute for Jared to introduce himself to Ruby, to make some irrelevant, meaningless, small talk—and then get straight to the point.

'Mum's pleased you're here.'

Dev nodded. 'You're not.'

'No. You'll just end up upsetting her.' His brother casually took a long sip of his beer.

'That's not the aim.'

Jared shrugged. Over Dev's shoulder he mouthed *hello!* at someone behind them. He was always so smooth—always so perfect. The perfect son—one of two both equally, differently perfect: at school, at sport, at socialising.

Then along came Dev. Not even close to perfect.

'You shouldn't have come,' he said, as friendly as if they were discussing a footy match. 'I wish you hadn't.' Now he bothered to catch his gaze. 'But as you're here, at least try not to ruin tonight for Mum, okay? It's her first party since...' Jared swallowed a few times, and the pain of his loss was clear even in the moonlight.

Dev reached out—but he didn't know what to do. So he let his hand flop back uselessly to his side. Jared was oblivious, his stare becoming hard.

'Just don't let her down again.' Jared pushed the words out between clenched teeth—and then wasted no time waiting for a response.

'Lovely to meet you,' he murmured to Ruby, and then Dev found his gaze following his brother's suit-jacketed shoulders as he walked away, across the limestone paving and back inside the house.

A hand brushed his arm. 'Dev?'

Ruby was looking up at him, questions in her eyes. 'You okay?'

He nodded sharply. 'Do you want a drink?'

She raised her eyebrows, but let him go. When he returned a few minutes later, she'd found a small bench nestled in the garden. A man he didn't recognise sat beside her, and something he said made her laugh. A beautiful, genuine, honest, Ruby laugh.

'She's with me,' he said, sounding about as caveman as he intended as he came to a stop before them.

The guy looked up and Dev could see the exact millisecond he realised who he was. And that was all it took—the man stood up without a word, and left.

Ruby looked at him disapprovingly as he sat. 'That was rude—and inaccurate.'

He handed her her champagne. 'It's what they all expect of me. And, also, it was technically correct. You did come with me.'

She smiled, just a little. 'That's not what you meant.'

He shrugged. 'I've got other things to worry about than some guy who doesn't have the guts to stand his ground.'

She took a sip of her drink, looking out across the garden. 'Yeah, I'm getting that feeling.' Another sip. 'Are you going to tell me about it?'

'No.'

She shifted on the wooden bench, and recrossed her long legs so they were angled towards him. 'Then why, exactly, did you bring me here tonight?'

'I don't think I know,' he said, deciding she deserved honesty—even if he couldn't provide answers.

I really don't want to go on my own.

That particular moment of honesty in Ruby's apartment had definitely been unplanned. Until that moment, even he hadn't known it was true. He'd told himself that she'd make the night more fun, that she'd be—his favourite word when it came to her, it seemed—a distraction.

Looking at her now, at her eyes that were wide with concern for him, *distraction* didn't really cut it.

Because Veronica could've organised him a distraction, a stunning accessory for his arm who wouldn't have asked a single question.

But he hadn't wanted that; he'd wanted Ruby. He'd used that stupid *favour*—something he'd dreamt up in some desperate attempt to gain control of a humiliating situation, a favour he'd never thought he'd use—to get her here.

He'd manipulated her—for the second time.

And once again, he just couldn't feel bad about it.

He was glad she was here. *Ruby.* Not anyone else.

'I heard that your father died,' she said, very softly. 'Someone mentioned it, on set.' A pause. 'I'm really sorry.'

'We weren't close,' he said, dismissive. 'The opposite, in fact.'

'I'm sorry,' she repeated.

'I didn't go to the funeral,' he said, suddenly. Unexpectedly.

'You couldn't make it?' she asked, and he liked that she'd jumped to that conclusion, as erroneous as it was.

'He wouldn't have wanted me there. You could say we didn't agree on a lot of things.'

An understatement.

Dev waited for her to judge him on that decision. To tell him he'd made a mistake.

'Is that why your brother is so angry with you?'

Dev managed a tight smile. 'Brothers. And yes, that's partly why. The rest has been a lifetime in the making.'

'You're the odd one out.'

A small, harsh laugh. 'Yeah.'

'Are you close to your mum?'

He nodded.

'But you haven't seen her much recently.' He must have looked at her curiously. 'She was shocked to see you tonight, I could tell. So I guessed you hadn't popped by for dinner in a while.'

'I haven't been here in years. Ten years or more. When I saw Mum, it was somewhere else. A restaurant or something.'

'Because of your dad?'

Another nod.

For a while they were both silent, and little snippets of unintelligible conversation drifted across the breeze to them.

'That really sucks, you know,' she said, finally. 'That you have siblings, parents—and you're estranged from them all.'

He knew what she meant. That she'd had none of that. No family to be estranged from.

'Sometimes I think it would've been better if I didn't have them.'

All he associated his family with were guilt and failure—his. And disappointment—theirs. Except for his mum—but then, she got the consolation prize of worrying about her youngest son all the time.

'Now that,' Ruby said, 'was a very stupid thing to say.'

Her matter-of-fact words made him blink. 'Pardon me?'

She didn't back down—but then, she never did.

'You heard me.'

She spoke without anger, and something—something about how sure she was of his apparent stupidity—made him smile.

'I like you, Ruby Bell.'

'You keep saying that.'

He stood up, holding out a hand for her. 'I think I just fig-ured out the reason I invited you.'

'Invited? Is that what you call it?'

But she was smiling as she wrapped her fingers around his. They were just slightly cool, but where they touched his skin they triggered instant heat.

'I reckon we go enjoy this party.'

Whatever Ruby might think, right now he didn't need to talk.

But then, he didn't want a mindless distraction either.

Quite simply, he wanted Ruby.

CHAPTER TEN

LATER—MUCH LATER—Ruby leant against the mirrored walls of the penthouse's private elevator, and grinned at Dev.

'That was fun,' she said. She felt good, buzzing with a touch of champagne, her toes pleasantly sore from hours of dancing.

'Yeah,' he said, with a slightly bemused smile. 'I know.'

The elevator doors slid open, and Ruby stepped out, her boot heels loud on the foyer's marble floor. A lamp on a spindly-legged side table glowed softly, only partially lighting the room.

But two steps later, she stopped dead.

'Where am I sleeping?'

Dev laughed behind her, and Ruby turned to look at him. He'd propped his shoulders against the wallpaper beside the shiny elevator door, and he looked at her with a sparkle to his eyes.

He pointed at the floor. 'I booked you a suite on the floor below.'

'What's so funny?' she asked. But the narrowing of her eyes was more a habit now. At some point he'd stopped being *quite* so irritating.

Come to think of it, for at least half the night—more if she disregarded the whole favour debacle—he'd been quite the opposite.

'This is a private elevator. You'll need to go all the way back to the lobby. When we arrived I didn't think.'

'Oh,' she said, nodding.

Dev didn't move. His jacket was thrown haphazardly over

his arm, and part of his shirt had untucked itself. He should look like a mess. Instead he looked…rather appealing.

Dishevelled. Yes. That was the word for it.

Ruby blinked, and attempted to refocus. She needed to go to her room.

As she walked to the elevator Dev didn't move. He just stayed where he was, looking at her with an unreadable expression.

She pushed the down button—the only button on the shiny brass panel.

And waited.

Not for the elevator door to open—as it did that immediately—but for…*something.*

The doors had opened fully now, and Ruby could see herself reflected in its walls. She looked into her own eyes, trying to determine what was going on here. Why she was still outside the elevator.

Her gaze wasn't so unsure though. Her gaze was…

The doors shut again, and now all she could see of herself was the blurriest of silhouettes.

'You're still here,' Dev said.

Out of the corner of her eye she knew he hadn't moved. But he was watching her. Waiting.

Now all she could hear was the sound of her own breathing—definitely faster than was normal.

She turned, a slow, deliberate movement.

And then Dev was there, standing right in front of her. *So close.*

She tilted her chin upwards to catch his gaze.

'I'm still here.' There was a long pause. 'You're very difficult to resist, you know that?'

His gaze, already warm, flickered hotter.

She reached out, her fingers toying with the untucked hem of his shirt, then travelling upwards, tracing his buttons in slow, irregular movements. 'Maybe it's the whole world-famous-movie-star thing.'

She felt him tense beneath her fingertips. 'Maybe,' he said. But his tone was flat.

Her exploration had reached his collar, skimming across its sharp, starched edge. Then she was touching skin: the cords of his neck. His jaw. Hot beneath her touch.

'Or maybe not,' she said. Then she looked up again, looked up into those blue, blue eyes.

Who was she looking at? At Devlin Cooper, Hollywood star? Or Dev, the man who made her heart flip, and who managed to make her smile just as regularly as he pushed her buttons? Who made her breath catch when he allowed her a glimpse of his true self? The man who'd calmly cleaned up her kitchen and who'd reached for her hand in his mother's front hall?

Could he tell that for her there really was no question?

Yes, she thought as he leant towards her, and as she stood on impatient tiptoes.

Yes, she thought as their lips finally met, and as he pulled her tight against him—and before the incredible touch of his mouth obliterated the possibility of any further thinking at all.

Dev woke, gradually. It was dark—very much night still.

As his eyes adjusted in the blackness, Ruby's shape materialised before him. She slept on her side, facing him. He liked the way the sheet followed her shape, up along the long length of her legs, over the roundness of her hips, then down to the dip of her waist.

She was asleep, her breathing slow and regular.

How long had he been asleep for?

He turned over, reaching for his phone on the bedside table. Pressing the button to make the screen illuminate simply confirmed what he'd suspected: it was two in the morning. He'd slept for less than an hour.

He bit back a groan. What had he expected? One visit to see his mum and suddenly life would be back to normal? He'd finally be able to sleep?

Well—yes. That was exactly it.

It was exactly why after all these weeks he'd finally sat down about twenty-four hours ago—once again unable to sleep—and listened to every single one of his mother's voicemail messages, no matter how much it hurt.

The decision to charter a flight and attend the party had come much later the next day, out of the blue. He hadn't questioned it at the time, nor his decision to take Ruby with him.

And he didn't regret either decision. Tonight had been...he didn't know. Something good. A step forward maybe.

To where he had no idea, but the sense of moving in any direction was certainly a welcome contrast to the past few months.

Except—he still couldn't sleep.

He wasn't magically cured.

It made him want to hit something.

Instead, he pushed himself off the bed in jerky, frustrated movements, and headed for the en suite. He shut the door carefully behind him before switching on the light, not wanting to wake Ruby.

Someone had ensured his zip-up bag of toiletry supplies had made it into the bathroom, and he barely had to look into it to find the familiar tray of tablets. A moment later he'd pushed a couple out onto his hand, but, rather than transferring them to his mouth, he found himself just staring at them.

He was reluctant to take them with Ruby here. They lasted a good five hours, and if Ruby tried to wake him before then he'd be groggy, a mess.

Last time she stayed with him, he'd lain on the couch, wanting to put distance between himself and Ruby. Then, after her aborted attempt to leave, he hadn't thought twice about his tablets. He'd known she'd be gone in the morning, and told himself he didn't care—that it was exactly what he wanted.

But tonight that option held no appeal. He didn't want to retreat to another room, and he didn't want to be a drugged-out lump beside her.

Was it so much to ask? A night where he got to be normal again? Where he could sleep beside a beautiful woman with only thoughts of *her* in his stupid head, and not useless things he could do nothing about?

He just wanted to sleep beside Ruby. To wake beside her and not feel as if the weight of the world were on his shoulders, or that getting out of bed was an impossible option.

He dropped the tablets into the sink, then twisted the tap so hot water chased them down the drain.

Decision made, he switched off the bathroom light, and climbed back beneath the sheets.

But once there, even the gentle in and out of Ruby's breathing proved no use.

Sleep was as elusive as always. Tonight was no different from the many nights before it.

Finally, hating himself, he surrendered—to the pills, and to the necessary oblivion of sleep.

Dev was still asleep when Ruby stepped out of the bathroom. She wrapped her arms around herself as she watched him, cosy in the thick terry-towelling robe she wore. He slept just as he had that morning—was it really only last week?—when she'd agreed to the silly deal that had landed her here. Which was like a log, basically.

Now what?

Briefly she considered repeating her exit from a fortnight earlier—and simply disappearing.

But this morning, that just didn't seem right. Or, at least not an option she was letting herself think too much about.

She'd get dressed, then figure out what would happen next. After all, that would fit the theme of the last twenty-four hours—making decisions without pretty much any thought of the consequences.

Her clothes were puddled on the floor, and as she bent to gather them in her arms her familiar red carry-on suitcase caught her attention. It lay on its back, right beside Dev's backpack, in front of a wardrobe.

Disappearing was suddenly a *very* viable option, she decided as she stalked on bare feet to their luggage.

Had he really even booked her another room? How dared he assume—?

But just before she snatched the bag up, an unevenly folded note drew her attention, balanced atop the red fabric.

She'd barely read the single handwritten sentence, when she heard a sleepy laugh behind her.

'I had the concierge organise for your bag to be brought up here after you fell asleep.'

Oh.

'I thought you might want your things.'

She turned to face him. He'd raised himself onto his elbows, the sheet falling low to reveal the delicious strength of his chest.

She glanced down at Dev's note again, his neat all-capitals script.

'Cross my heart,' he added, into her continued silence.

She believed him—that wasn't the issue. It was just taking her a moment to absorb the thoughtfulness of the gesture— firstly that he'd thought to organise for her bag to be delivered, and secondly that he knew her well enough to guess her reaction at the bag's discovery.

It felt...nice.

'Thanks,' she said.

He rubbed at his eyes, his movements slow and heavy-look- ing. 'How does breakfast in bed sound? Room service here is exceptional.'

And just like that, she'd decided what she was doing next.

They ended up spending the day in Sydney.

With no driver—and Dev in dark glasses and a baseball cap—they headed for Bondi beach.

Ruby had pointed out an advertisement as she'd read the paper, the many Sunday sections spread like giant colourful confetti across the bed. *Sculpture by the Sea.*

Dev couldn't say he was a regular visitor to art exhibitions, but he figured he could do a lot worse than walking from Bondi along the coast down to Tamarama—with Ruby. So yeah, he was sold.

It was a mild October day, and yet keen sunbathers still dotted the beach. They both held their shoes in their hands as they walked, the sand smooth beneath their feet and the ocean as perfect a blue as the sky.

'Where's the art?' Dev asked.

Ruby smiled and pointed vaguely ahead of them, the slight breeze ruffling her hair. 'I think it starts down there somewhere?'

But really, neither of them was too worried about the sculptures.

During the short drive from the city, they'd chatted easily—a continuation of their easy breakfast picnic-of-sorts on his bed. It all stayed very light, which suited him just fine.

No talk about anything serious. No talk about last night, and certainly no talk about tomorrow.

But now, in Bondi, they'd gone quiet.

Not an awkward silence—quite the opposite. But still, Dev didn't like it.

'What's your favourite movie?' Ruby said—all in a rush, as if maybe she didn't like the silence either. 'I mean, of yours. That you've been in.'

As she walked she stared at a spot somewhere on the sand ahead of her.

'*Now You See Her*,' he said, immediately.

She looked up at him, her eyes squinting a little in the glare. 'I've never heard of it.' She paused a second. 'Sorry.'

He smiled. 'Good. It's awful. I had about two lines in it, a straight-to-video effort filmed on the Gold Coast when I was twenty.'

'And so it's your favourite because?'

'I got paid for it. My first paid role in a movie.'

They'd reached the end of the beach and paused to step back into their shoes before walking up a small ramp to the footpath.

'That's interesting,' she said. 'Not your first starring role, or first blockbuster, or first Golden Globe nomination?'

'Nope. It was the money in my bank account—as small amount as it was. Proved it wasn't just a dream—but that it could be my career.'

They walked a little further without speaking, past the famous Bondi Icebergs swimming club. Dev had been here a few times—not to swim in a pool so close to the ocean that the Pacific's waves often broke straight into it, but to the bar. For a few promotional events, the occasional dinner...

Irrationally he imagined coming back here with Ruby, in summer, to swim. For a moment he could almost see it—her hair slicked back just as it had been after her shower this morning, smiling at him across the water...

But he quickly erased that idea—he wouldn't be in Australia in summer, he'd be in Hollywood.

By then, everything would be back to how it was. And Ruby would be off working on her next film, along with all her rules about dating cast and crew, and her refusal to ever settle down in one location.

'Dev?'

Ruby had asked him a question, he realised. 'Sorry, I was...' He ran a hand through his hair. 'What did you say?'

'I was worried I'd offended you,' she said. 'Don't worry, it was a stupid question.'

He slanted her a look. 'You do know you have to ask me it now?'

But they'd reached a little temporary marquee—the start of the sculpture walk. A few minutes later, equipped with a catalogue, they'd descended a series of stairs to reach the first set of sculptures, scattered across the tiers of rocks that lined the cove and spread their way into the ocean.

Ruby stood in front of one—a giant red nail that appeared to have been hammered between the rocks, tall enough to loom above them both.

'What was your question?'

She sighed. 'It was nothing. I was just saying I was surprised that the money meant so much to you.'

'Given my background,' he finished for her.

She shifted her weight awkwardly. 'As I said, a stupid thing to say.'

'I'm not that easily offended,' he said. At least, not with her. But then—if she was someone interviewing him—he never would've answered the original question honestly, anyway.

Actually, he wasn't entirely sure he'd told anyone the truth before.

Not that it meant anything—it was a trivial thing. Meaningless.

'Having a privileged background doesn't mean I don't have an appreciation for hard work, or for money.'

'Of course not,' she said, very quickly.

He knew he could've left it at that, but as they walked further along the path he found himself explaining. 'My dad was a self-made man,' he said.

Ruby didn't say anything, but her pace slowed.

'He started with absolutely nothing—as a labourer, actually. Mum met him back then. He worked his way up, he became a builder. Then began his own construction business, and started to buy and sell property. Sometimes to renovate and sell, other times to hold, or to rent.'

They'd walked straight past the next sculpture, Dev realised. But he didn't want to stop; if he did, the words would, too.

'All he wanted for us boys was security. A secure career. A good income. A good family.'

'So he didn't want you to be an actor,' she said.

He lips quirked, but it wasn't a smile. 'No.'

Ruby didn't even glance at the next sculpture. Stairs rose above them, leading out of the cove, and they walked up side by side, Ruby's fingers brushing against the hand rail.

'I was supposed to be an accountant.'

'No!' Ruby said, and it was such an exclamation that Dev had to grin.

'That's what I thought, too. I wasn't as good at school as my brothers—Dad said it was because I didn't apply myself, and he was probably right. I just didn't like sitting still, I didn't like being quiet and studying in my room.'

'I believe that,' Ruby murmured. 'I bet you were a trouble-maker, too.'

'Yeah,' he said, smiling fondly at a million memories. 'Dad didn't like that, either.'

To their right, greenery and grass reached up to the road above them. Tiny painted totem poles decorated the slope—but Dev wasn't really paying any attention.

'So, yeah, earning my first pay cheque meant something. A lot.'

She nodded. 'Your dad must have been pleased.'

'I doubt it. I'd moved out by then.'

She looked at him, with questions in her eyes—and as they walked he found himself telling her everything. About that night when his dad had been waiting for him; when he'd been drunk—and arrogant; when he'd felt the crunch of his father's fist against his cheek.

How he'd never gone back.

Ruby just listened, letting him talk.

'You were right the first time,' he said, after a while. 'About your surprise that a wealthy kid would appreciate a pay cheque so much. Six months earlier, I wouldn't have. I *was* spoilt. I did take my life for granted. I'd never have admitted it—maybe because I didn't even realise it—but deep down I *knew* I had a safety net. I'd subconsciously given myself the option to fail.'

The footpath ended, and grassy flat parkland spread before them. Large pieces of abstract art—some whimsical, some just bizarre—attracted groups of people. A pride of lions made out of what looked like straw; a delicately balanced collection of chairs topped with two metallic acrobats, and even an over-sized mixer tap.

'But you didn't fail,' she said.

'I couldn't,' he said.

No way would he let his dad be right.

'So you did achieve what your father wanted for you: a career, financial security.'

'Not the way he wanted.'

They'd left the park, the footpath leading them to another cove, the blue-green waves splashing across tiers of huge, smooth rocks.

'Did that matter?'

He didn't know. That was the problem, *his* problem.

And now it was too late.

So he didn't answer the question. They just walked, and Ruby didn't ask again. They followed the edge of the ocean, in silence, until they hit the white sand of Tamarama beach. Ruby quickened her pace a little, and led him between sculptures— finally flopping cross-legged beside a giant turtle constructed of tyre rubber.

He sat beside her, his legs stretched out, the sand warm beneath his skin.

'A miscarriage,' she said, out of the blue.

'Pardon me?'

She was looking at the ocean. Surfers bobbed just beyond the cresting waves.

'Yesterday you asked what happened. And that's it. What made me take my life in a less scandalous direction.'

There was a deliberate lightness to her words that she didn't come close to pulling off.

'I'm sorry, Ruby.'

She nodded. 'Thank you. I'd been seeing this guy—a nice guy. From a good family, very smart, very handsome. He had his choice of anyone. I wouldn't say he chose me, though. Or at least, he didn't mean to.'

Dev held his tongue, although it was near impossible.

'It was an accident, me getting pregnant. I hadn't meant it to happen, although of course that isn't what people said.'

People. People gossiping about Ruby, judging her.

She shifted a little on the sand, so she faced him. 'But I

was *so* happy. I didn't expect it, but it was like—' she bit her lip, looking down for a moment '—like finally I'd have a family. I didn't care if it was just me and my baby, but then the father surprised everyone and decided to stay with me. He was a good guy.'

She was tracing a hand through the sand, drawing illegible scribbles that instantly faded away.

'So I had everything: my baby, a guy. It was perfect. Finally I felt like I had a purpose. That I belonged. I wasn't the girl who people whispered about, I was going to be a *mother,* and I had a boyfriend who said he'd stand by me. A *family.*'

Her hand moved from the sand, to her stomach. Somehow Dev knew she was unaware of what she was doing, the way her fingers lay across the perfectly flat line of her T-shirt.

'I was stupid, and I told people as soon as I knew. I was showing off, I guess. Over-excited—proving them all wrong. I never considered the possibility of miscarrying, and I certainly didn't understand how common it was so early in a pregancy. And then one day I started bleeding, and when I went to the hospital they told me I'd lost my baby. I felt like my world had ended.'

He couldn't just sit still any more. He reached for her, wrapping his arm around her waist and pulling her close against him. She pressed her cheek against his chest.

'That's when I figured it out—figured out that I had it all wrong. I dumped the guy—a relief for him I'm sure—and quit my dead-end job to go back to school. I decided I was all I needed in my life—that I didn't need some guy, or a family, or *anyone,* to be happy. I just needed me.'

She was so sure, her voice so firm.

But her body shook, just a little.

She tilted her chin up, to look at him, finally.

He didn't know what to say. Or maybe he knew that there wasn't anything he could say, anything that would make a difference.

Besides, that wasn't what she wanted. It wasn't what he'd wanted, either, when he'd told her about his dad.

So he did the only thing that did make sense—and kissed her.

But it was different from their kisses of before—this wasn't flirty, although it was certainly passionate. It was...beautiful, and sad, and he was suddenly *sure* there was something different between them, some connection, something special. And he was the last guy to think anything as fluffy and romantic as that.

But with Ruby, on the beach, beneath the sun and beside the giant friendly tortoise, it was unlike anything he'd ever experienced.

'Oh, my *God,* it's *Dev Cooper!*'

The shriek tore them apart. Immediately Ruby retreated, shrugging off his arm in a brutal motion, and jumping to her feet.

He glanced up to see a group of teenage girls approaching him, all pointing and chattering loudly. Across the beach people were twisting on their towels to have a look, to see what all the fuss was about.

Earlier today he'd seen a few curious, wondering glances, but he'd been lucky. No one had approached him, no one had burst the little bubble that he and Ruby had so inadvertently created. After a while he'd stopped even noticing, he'd been so wrapped up in Ruby.

But that bubble was gone now—destroyed. Ruby was looking back towards the houses and the road above the beach, as if determining her escape strategy.

Not from the rapidly approaching crowd—but from him.

He was on his feet. 'Ruby—'

She had her phone in her hand. 'I'll sort out a car. You won't be able to walk back to Bondi, now.'

Not *we won't,* but *you.*

She spoke in her work voice, as professional and false as it got.

And as the girls slowed their charge to look at him almost shyly, momentarily lost for words, his pasted-on smile was equally plastic.

But then he *was* a good actor, so he submitted to the autographs, and the photos, and the screaming—while the whole time all he wanted to do was to yell and shout and tell them all to go away. To leave him alone.

Although even if they did it would be too late. Ruby was only metres away, her arms wrapped around herself, watching.

But that moment had passed. Their moment.

He told himself it was for the best, that it wasn't something he wanted, or needed.

Just like Ruby, he'd long ago made his own path.

And he walked it alone.

CHAPTER ELEVEN

ON MONDAY EVENING, Ruby nosed her hire car up the long gravel driveway to Dev's cottage. Even as she pulled to a stop she wasn't entirely sure what she was doing.

She'd been driving home from another long day, already planning what she was going to order at the pub for dinner. And then—unexpectedly—she was here.

No. That wasn't completely true.

It wasn't at all unexpected. Given the amount of time her subconscious had allocated to Dev today, her arrival here could even be considered foreseeable.

That fact didn't make it any less a bad idea.

She held the car key in her hand, and made a half-hearted attempt to reach for the ignition before stopping herself.

She was here now. She might as well go talk to him—clear the air.

Yesterday's flight home had been awkward. There was no other word for it. It was obvious neither of them had intended what had happened at the beach.

She should regret it, she knew. Why would she share something so personal with a man she barely knew?

A few times, during that long hour in the jet, she'd meant to say something. To somehow laugh off what had happened.

But it was impossible. She couldn't very well tell him: *Look, I've never told anyone else—ever—what I told you today. Just forget it, okay?*

Right.

Last night she'd lain in bed, telling herself she'd made the sensible decision to back away. That her immediate reaction to that dose of reality—as shocking as if someone had dumped a bucket of salt water on top of her—was appropriate.

He was *Devlin Cooper.* She needed to remember that. It was so easy to be seduced into reading something more into the situation, imagining so much more than there was between them, or would ever be.

He wasn't looking for for ever, and she certainly didn't want it.

So today, her mind had wandered for the hundredth time to little flashbacks of how Dev had looked as he'd leant against the wall beside the elevator; or the way he'd looked at her, that moment before he'd kissed her, down at Tamarama...

She shoved open her door, stepping out into the cool evening.

Belatedly she realised the front door was now open. Dev stood, propped against the doorframe, watching her.

Waiting for her.

'Looked like you were doing some serious thinking there,' he said as she stepped onto the veranda.

'No,' she lied, quickly. 'Quite the opposite. I was thinking we've been spending way too much time being serious.'

His lips quirked. 'How so?' he asked, a little gruffly.

Where he stood, half in the shadows and half illuminated by the hallway light, she couldn't read his gaze.

She stepped closer, attempting what she hoped was a flirtatious, happy-go-lucky, I'm-totally-cool-about-all-this smile.

He took a step backwards, gesturing for her to come in.

But she didn't. She needed to get this sorted first. They needed to both understand what this was.

'Maybe you were right,' she said. Dev raised his eyebrows. 'A few weeks ago, outside the pub. When you said we were just two single people stuck in a country town. How did you put it? A match made in heaven.'

He nodded. 'You said you didn't date anyone you worked with.'

'Too late now,' she said, with a bit of a laugh. 'Besides, some-how we've flown under the radar. No gossip.'

'Except for Graeme. Graeme thinks you're great, by the way. You should hear him on our drives into set.'

Ruby smiled. 'Well, then, Graeme is very discreet. I'll have to thank him.'

They both fell into silence.

'So what you're saying is?' Dev prompted.

Ruby narrowed her eyes. 'Isn't it obvious?'

'Not at all,' he said. But was that a sparkle in his eyes?

She gave a little huff of frustration. 'Fine.' And she closed the gap between them, and before she had the chance to lose her nerve—and just because she wanted to—she kissed him.

Not tentatively, not questioning.

When, after an age, they broke apart, she needed to take a few long breaths to pull herself together.

'That's what I want,' she said.

He was reaching for her again. 'I like this plan.'

'Just until the film is over,' she clarified as he almost carried her inside, slamming the front door behind them.

Maybe it was the sound of the door, or the distraction of Dev kissing her neck, and the shiver it triggered through her body—but her words weren't as firm, or as clear, as she'd like.

But she didn't have a chance to repeat them, as now Dev had swept her up into his arms and was carrying her to his room.

And really, now wasn't the time for talking.

Ruby had dinner with him every night, and they took advantage of all the food in his fridge—which magically doubled in volume, thanks to Graeme.

It was easy, and fun. He continued to pay her no special attention on set, although it was difficult. Especially when Ruby broke her own rules—just once—when delivering an updated copy of the day's script.

It had been a genuine, work-related visit—but the kiss behind his very firmly closed trailer door was far from professional.

The memory made him smile as he stretched out along his couch. Ruby walked back from the kitchen, a glass of red wine in her hand.

'Now don't you look comfortable?'

He smiled, and tapped the space in front of him on the striped fabric. Her eyes sparkled as she sipped her wine, then placed the glass carefully on the coffee table.

She came into his arms easily. How long had it been now—a week? A week since she'd turned up at his front door, still with her rules, but with him, and this film, a temporary exception.

But he could live with this, especially when she kissed him. When Ruby was kissing him, *that* was all he thought about, all that filled his mind.

But when she left—and she always did—then he would think.

She'd leave around midnight. Ruby said it was because sometimes she gave members of the crew lifts to set—which sounded plausible.

But it wasn't the real reason. She was keeping this light, and simple. Waking up together, or breakfast in bed, or conversations where they bared their souls—no. They were not things they wanted, not what this thing they had was about.

They both knew that.

Did she guess he still wasn't sleeping? Sometimes he thought so. She'd look at him with concern in her eyes, and occasionally he'd be sure she was going to start asking questions.

But she never did.

On set, the rumours had dissipated. Dev had done nothing to perpetuate them—excluding that one morning, he'd never missed his call, had never been anything but prompt and professional. Everyone seemed to love Dev Cooper.

And, thank goodness, there were no *new* rumours. This was Ruby's nightmare, the niggling fear at the back of her mind that suddenly All Would Be Revealed somehow, or that the paparazzi that occasionally bothered to make the trip out to Lucyville would snap a photo of her and Dev together.

Which would be difficult—given their relationship existed entirely within the walls of his cottage. Graeme got rid of any loitering cars anywhere near the property, and so far it was proving remarkably effective.

But still—Ruby worried.

And not just about becoming the subject of gossip once again, but about Dev.

She needed to go. She lay curled on his couch, her back to Dev's chest, a warm blanket covering them both. Earlier they'd been watching a nineteen-fifties Danny Kaye musical they both loved—but not enough to be rather easily distracted. It had long ago ended, the TV screen now black.

Dev was breathing steadily behind her, but she knew he wasn't asleep. She seemed to have a talent for dozing off, but not Dev. Except for that morning in the penthouse, she'd never seen him sleep. Not once.

He mustn't be sleeping. Not well, anyway. She knew that whenever she saw the red in his eyes and his skin after he washed off his day's stage make-up. She'd seen a packet of sleeping tablets in his bathroom, but she had no idea if he took them. She'd never asked.

She'd never asked about anything.

She could guess what was wrong. Extrapolate from what he'd told her at the beach that day. All the rumours had been way off. Her guess was that Dev was still processing his father's death, and his own grief. That was the cause of his weight loss, his problems sleeping, the sadness in his gaze.

But that was all it was—a guess. So many times she was tempted to ask him about it. Like right now, in this darkened room, and in this intimacy they shared.

Did he want to talk to her about it? Did he want to share something so personal with her?

Did she want him to share something so personal?

No.

On the beach, it had all been too intense. Too much, too over-whelming. He'd felt the same way, too.

She didn't want that. She couldn't want that—not when they had only weeks together.

What would be the point?

So she turned in his arms and kissed him goodbye. And, as she did every other night, drove home to her own, lonely bed.

And she told herself she was doing the right thing.

Ruby woke up with a start, blinking in the unfamiliar room.

Dev's place.

She'd fallen asleep. Her handbag was still out in the lounge room, so she turned over, planning to reach across Dev to where she knew he left his phone on his beside table, so she could check the time.

But Dev wasn't there.

She crawled across the bed, wrapping herself with a sheet before she checked his phone. Three-twelve a.m.

Far too late to drive back to her place.

She realised she didn't mind.

A thin crack of light glowed beneath the en-suite door. 'Dev?'

No response. She stood, arranging the sheet like a towel. She felt faintly ridiculous for her sudden modesty—Dev had, after all, seen her naked.

But still, just walking about his house in the nude felt like a step too far—a dose of reality in their perfect little world.

She knocked on the door, but the slight touch pushed it open.

Dev sat on the closed toilet lid, in boxer shorts only. His head had been in his hands, and as he looked up at her he raked his fingers through his hair, making one side stand up on end.

He looked—awful. Worse than she'd ever seen him, despite the much-needed weight she'd noticed he'd put on in the past few weeks.

The shadows beneath his eyes were verging on black, and his eyes were rimmed red.

He looked exhausted. Broken. Ruined.

Of course it wasn't a surprise.

But she'd made herself ignore it. She hadn't wanted to know.

It didn't fit with what she'd decided was allowable between them. This was far, far too serious.

'Oh, Dev...'

She went to his side, automatically wrapping her arm around his shoulder. She crouched awkwardly beside the cistern but didn't care. She had to do something.

But he shrugged her off.

'I'm fine,' he said, angrily. Much louder than she expected. It made her want to back away, but she didn't let herself.

'No,' she said, 'you're not.'

He looked away—at the towel rail. At nothing.

'I'm just having trouble sleeping,' he said, all dismissive. 'That's all.'

She glanced at the sink. A tray of tablets lay almost empty on the counter top.

'It's not good for you to use those for too long,' she began.

He stood up abruptly, crossing the room. 'I *know* that,' he said. He was looking at himself in the mirror, as if he hated what he saw.

Ruby straightened, but didn't go to him.

'Without them I just don't sleep. I can't.'

'Okay.'

He looked at her, his gaze unbelievably intense. 'If I don't take them, I don't sleep. And if I don't sleep, I can't—'

Act.

He snatched at something. Two tablets, she realised, sitting on the ceramic counter.

Right in her line of sight. As if he'd been staring at them.

For how long?

He tossed them at his mouth, then wrenched the tap on, gathering water in his cupped hands that he tipped haphazardly down his throat.

Everything inside her screamed at her to leave.

She'd decided she didn't want this. This was supposed to be fun, and flirty, and temporary.

Nothing that was happening right now was *any* of those things.

'Can you please leave?' he said, meeting her gaze in the mirror.

Because he asked, she nodded.

But she didn't go very far. Not to her car, and certainly not back home to her apartment.

Instead, she shut the bathroom door behind her, and crawled straight back into Dev's bed.

She didn't know what she was doing, or what she could offer him.

But tonight, she was not walking away.

After Ruby left, Dev spent long minutes in the bathroom, waiting for his whirring brain to slow.

He'd known she hadn't meant to stay, but when she had, he'd been glad.

Really glad.

Stupid, really.

Because what did it matter? Filming ended in two weeks, and then he'd fly back to LA. And Ruby would... He didn't even know. *That* was how transient this relationship was.

But even so, he'd tried again. Tried to sleep like a normal person. To fall asleep beside Ruby.

Predictably, just like last week in that fancy penthouse, sleep hadn't come. But tonight he'd really resisted the tablets.

Tonight he'd thought it might be different.

Why?

Just like how the mornings hadn't been any different? The one single variation from the murky fog that was his mornings was last Sunday, when he'd woken beside Ruby. And even that had only worked because he'd been fortunate she'd slept in so late. He'd been nearly normal.

He'd hoped that would become the norm, but it hadn't. Nights were hard. Mornings even worse. It was a constant, awful cycle of frustration—and in between he managed to be to all appearances a fully functional human being.

A miracle, probably, that on this film at least he could hide whatever the hell was wrong with him. He could hide it from Ruby.

Until tonight. Tonight he'd done a really crap job of hiding it.

He didn't think Ruby would be coming back tomorrow night. This wasn't what she'd signed up for.

He pushed the door open, not bothering to switch off the light. The bathroom light flooded the room, and the obvious feminine shape on the bed.

For a minute or more he just stood there, then gave his increasingly blurry head a shake, and switched off the light.

In the gloom he slid onto his side of the bed, and without letting himself think too much—and quite frankly with the drugs unable to do much thinking anyway—he reached for her.

She wasn't asleep, he realised, and she turned to face him in his arms.

'I'm fine,' he whispered into her hair.

'I want you to be,' she said, her breath tickling his chest.

And then his eyes slid shut, but a moment before the thick blackness of drugged sleep enveloped him he made a decision.

Tomorrow things would change. Not because he'd crossed his fingers or shouted into his brain that it would, but because he'd just lied to Ruby.

And he didn't want to do that again.

I want you to be.

Finally, he slept.

CHAPTER TWELVE

LATE ON WEDNESDAY afternoon—two days later—Dev knocked on his mother's front door. He shoved his hands in the pockets of his jeans to stop himself fidgeting, but it was a pretty useless gesture.

He was nervous.

He'd chartered another jet, and the entire flight he'd bounced his legs, or tapped his toes or *something.* Now he turned around on the spot, looking out onto the manicured front garden and his nondescript hire car, taking deep, relaxing breaths.

This really wasn't a big deal. It was his mum, and—despite everything—he knew she loved him.

Behind him the door rattled—the sound of the brass chain lock being undone, the click of the deadbolt, the twist of the door handle.

By the time the door opened, he was staring at it, waiting.

'Devlin!' his mum exclaimed, once again with a smile broader than he deserved. Then she paused. 'Is everything okay?'

She looked momentarily stricken, and he wanted to kick himself. Was a disaster the only reason she could imagine him visiting her unannounced?

Well, given the past fourteen years—probably.

'Everything's fine. Everyone's fine, as far as I know.'

She nodded, then opened the door wide. 'Well, come in! I was just going through the photos from my party. It was so wonderful to have you there.'

He nodded automatically, then reached out, grabbing his mum's hand and holding it tight.

'Mum, I'd like to talk to you about Dad.'

Instantly he saw the pain in her eyes, but she squeezed his fingers tighter.

'Good,' she said. 'Because I've got something I want to show you.'

Dev had cancelled dinner last night, and as Ruby walked to his front door late on Wednesday evening she wasn't sure what to expect.

Tuesday morning had been…eye-opening. When his alarm went off Dev just kept on sleeping, and it wasn't until she'd given him a decent shake that he'd finally woken.

He'd looked unhappy to see her, though. As if he'd wished the night had never happened, that she'd never seen him like that.

She'd felt like such an idiot, as the final pieces of the puzzle had fallen into place. That morning a few weeks back when she and Graeme had nearly bashed the front door down, Dev hadn't been sleeping in. He hadn't been so arrogant to believe his needs were more important than the rest of the cast and crew.

Something serious was going on with Dev, and she'd been at first oblivious—and then later deliberately dismissive—of the signs.

She'd been scared by how close she'd felt herself get to him, so she'd kept her distance.

Yeah, that was the word: scared.

But now what was she to do? All she could offer him was two more weeks. That was all she had. And she desperately wanted to help.

Now wasn't that a contradiction? So worried for Dev her heart ached, but so sure she had to leave.

He'd left the front door ajar, so she pushed it open, her heeled boots loud on the hallway's floorboards.

'Dev?'

He called out from the kitchen, and so that was where she

headed. He sat at the rustic dining table, cutlery, a bottle of wine and two glasses set out neatly. On his placemat only, however, lay a battered-looking notebook. He stood as she walked into the room.

'What's all this for?' she asked, taking in the soft lighting, and the scent of something delicious bubbling on the stove.

'I cooked,' he said, then added when she must have displayed her scepticism, 'Really. I make a mean puttanesca.'

She smiled, his enthusiasm completely infectious. 'Lucky me.'

He bent to kiss her, his lips firm. It was more than a quick hello kiss, and when they broke apart Ruby's heart was racing. Without thinking she brought her hand to her chest, and his lips quirked at the gesture.

'Me, too,' he said.

Dev wouldn't let her help as he confidently moved about the kitchen, so she propped a hip against the bench, and watched him as she sipped her wine.

They chatted about the day on set—about the temporary disaster of Arizona falling off the horse she was riding, the director's latest tantrum, and even the glorious cool but sunny weather.

But not the little notebook on the table.

Ruby would glance at it every so often, and after a while Dev grinned. 'I was going to explain while we ate—but you can go grab it if you like.'

She didn't need to be asked twice.

She sat at the dining table, facing Dev. But he'd slowed right down, his gaze regularly flicking in her direction.

The notebook had a brown leather cover, with Dev's surname embossed in a corner. Ruby ran a finger over it, already sure she knew who it once belonged to.

'It's your dad's, right?'

Dev nodded, but he kept his eyes focused on the pot he stirred.

Ruby opened the book. The first page was covered in numbers and dollar symbols. As was the next. A quick flick through the entire book showed it was nearly full with almost identical pages—dollar amounts. Some huge. Tens of millions of dollars. Hundreds of millions.

'What is this?'

Dev was carrying two plates piled high with pasta to the table. He placed them down carefully, then waited until he was in his seat before looking at Ruby—straight into her eyes, his gaze crystal clear.

'All I wanted, growing up, was for my dad to be proud of me.'

His voice cracked a little, and Ruby wanted to reach for him, but knew, instinctively, that now wasn't the time.

Dev swallowed. 'A cliché, I know. When I failed at that as a kid, I told myself I'd stopped caring what he thought. I used to tell myself that I wanted to become an actor because Dad would hate it, not because, deep down, I knew I was good at it. And that maybe, eventually, he'd see that.'

He kept twirling his fork, the same strands of pasta wrapping tighter and tighter.

'But he didn't. Then I left, and that was that. No more caring what Dad thought about me, no more looking to him for praise and approval. Except, then he went and died. And I realised that was all absolute crap. I've been waiting fourteen years to speak to my dad.'

'You still cared what he thought.'

Dev nodded, but then shook his head. 'Kind of. Of course I still wanted the slap on the back, the *good job, son,* all that stuff. But most of all, I just wanted to hear his voice. He worked so hard to achieve his goals, and he reached every single one. I should've swallowed my pride.'

His tone was so different from that afternoon on the beach. Now he spoke with near reverence—it was such a contrast. 'He could've called you, too,' Ruby pointed out. 'You're his son just as much as he's your father.'

Dev smiled. 'Of course he should've. But he was a stubborn old guy. Mum said he never even considered calling me.

Or coming with her when I visited. But then, I was exactly the same. As stubborn as him.'

He reached across the table, and took the notebook that was still in Ruby's hands. 'You know what this is? It's the takings at the box office for each of my movies. Every single one, right from that stupid one up at the Gold Coast that bombed. If he could find how much I was paid, that's there, too.'

He flipped through the pages, running his fingers over the print.

'Isn't that a little…?' Ruby struggled to find the right word.

'Harsh? Brutal? Mercenary? Yes. But that's Dad. That's what he understood: cold, hard cash. He could relate to that in a way he couldn't relate to my career.'

'Doesn't it bother you that this is what he focused on?'

Dev handed her back the book. Ruby opened it on a new page, now understanding the scribbled letters and numbers. It was meticulous: the box office takings across the world, DVD sales—everything.

This wasn't something thrown together in minutes—it was hours of work. Hours of research over months—years even. Crossing out numbers, updating them, adding them together.

'No,' she said, answering her own question.

'No,' he repeated.

'I went to a doctor today,' Dev said, later, in bed.

Ruby's back was to him, his body wrapped around hers.

She was silent, long enough that he thought she might have fallen asleep.

'Yes?' she said, eventually.

Her head was tucked beneath his chin, and her blonde hair smelt like cake, or cookies. *Vanilla-scented shampoo,* she'd told him, when he'd asked.

He hadn't been going to tell her this. Stupid, really, when he'd told her all that other stuff.

He hadn't even told his mum. He'd driven straight from his doctor's appointment in the city to the house where he'd grown up. Not on the advice of the GP, but because he'd planned on doing it anyway.

He'd made his decision the night before. Things had to change—*he* had to change—and no one but Devlin Cooper could do it.

'He thinks I could be depressed,' he said. Then he said the rest much more quickly, before he second-guessed himself silent. Ruby deserved to know. 'The trouble sleeping, the loss of appetite, the horrible mornings, it's all textbook, apparently.'

Had she tensed in his arms?

'I thought depression was…I don't know. When people lock themselves in their house all day. Can't work, can't function, can't…feel.' Her words were very soft, almost muffled in the sheets.

'It can be, I guess. My doctor explained the different types to me, and their symptoms. It just all fits, and the cause is pretty damn obvious. To be honest, I'm not all that surprised.'

She turned, pulling herself up a bit in the bed so her head rested on her pillow and she faced him. It was late, but enough moonlight filtered through the curtains for Dev to make out her expression; for once it was completely unreadable.

His palm felt cool against the fitted sheet, no longer touching her.

'I knew something was wrong, right from when I first met you.'

She reached for him, tracing the line of his jaw, across to his lips.

'I should've asked more questions, I should've pushed harder.'

Dev blinked, confused. 'I wouldn't have said anything. Not until now.'

She shook her head against the pillow, and carried on as if he'd never spoken. Her touch reached the fragile skin beneath his eyes, just as she had in his mother's library. 'I ignored this. I went back to my place each night *knowing* something was wrong.'

'You didn't do anything wrong,' he said. 'You *did* ask, but it wasn't the right time for me to say anything. No time was right.'

Her fingers fluttered away from his skin, and she twisted her hands awkwardly together in front of herself.

'I'm sorry,' she said.

He smiled, but she was too busy staring at her hands to notice. 'Don't be. I used to call you my distraction. I did feel when I was with you.'

In different ways. To start with it was very simple, very basic: lust. The thrill of the chase. His competitive nature to win the girl who rejected him.

But it was still heady, still an abrupt contrast to the beigeness of the rest of his days—and certainly the blackness of his nights.

And even her presence hadn't been enough to take him away from that.

But later, maybe even the first time she'd been in this room— when she'd been willing to do *anything* to get her job done, to get him to set—what he *felt* had shifted.

Oh, the lust was still there. There was something about Ruby, something about her smile, her laugh, her eyes...

But now there was more. Now there were moments of quiet that were the opposite of awkward. Times he looked at her and felt more connected to her than he could ever remember being with anyone. More comfortable but simultaneously completely off balance by his lack of familiarity with the emotions he felt around her.

'A distraction,' Ruby said, very, very softly.

Automatically he reached for her, but she moved, and his hand slid from her hip. 'In the very best possible way.'

Her lips curved into somewhat of a smile, and he knew he'd made a mistake.

'You're more than that, you're—'

But she cut him off.

'So what happens next?'

He needed a moment to refocus. 'With my depression?'

Her gaze flicked towards the ceiling. So she didn't like that word. He was the opposite—the label, in its own way, was powerful.

'The doctor gave me some pamphlets to read, and told me to have a think about it, and we'll meet again in a few weeks' time.'

'When *The Land* wraps.'

'Yeah,' he said.

'That sounds…'

'Anti-climactic?' Dev said, and she nodded. 'Kind of. We talked for a while, and even though I'd already decided to visit my mum, what he said just made it even more obvious. Depression is the symptom—I needed to resolve the cause.'

'And you think you have?'

Dev shifted his weight a little. 'Maybe. I hope so.'

Would he sleep tonight? He had no idea.

He expected Ruby to ask more questions, but she didn't. Instead they just lay there together, not touching.

More than anything he wanted to touch her, to pull her close against him again.

But if he did, she'd leave. He could as good as hear her excuses in his head.

It made no sense, none at all.

But Dev wanted her here, even at arm's length—so he didn't reach for her, and he didn't say a word.

And, eventually, he slept.

Ruby didn't sleep. She might've dozed, just a little, but mostly she just lay there, watching him.

Could it really be that easy? One visit to his mum, one battered leather notebook—and Dev was all better?

She didn't believe it.

Something had changed, though. A switch flipped, a corner turned…something like that. Not once tonight had she glimpsed a bleakness in Dev. No more little moments where he'd leave her, leave whatever they'd been doing, and retreat to wherever it was where his sadness, his regret, his guilt and his doubts lay. A weight had lifted.

She *was* happy for him. Thrilled. For him. Watching him sleep like this—*really* sleep, a true, natural sleep—was kind of wonderful.

No, just straight wonderful. Now she knew what she'd seen before, that drugged nothingness masquerading as restfulness—and the difference was undeniable.

What confused her was how *she* felt.

She felt restless, and she fidgeted as she attempted to sleep, her legs tangling in the quilt.

Finally she gave in to the compulsion to move, and climbed out of bed, walking on silent feet out of the room to avoid disturbing Dev. In the kitchen she automatically poured herself a glass of water, but she didn't drink it—just set it down on the granite bench top and walked away.

Her laptop sat on the dining-room table, from when she'd needed to make some changes to the script for Paul. She settled in front of it, flipping it open and blinking at the sudden brightness of the screen in the darkened room. She'd barely noticed the darkness, the moonlight flooding through the open kitchen blinds more than enough illumination for her to find her way.

She reopened an email that had arrived yesterday. A contact in London, who'd recommended her for a role. A great role, on a huge movie—big budget, already one confirmed big-name star.

She had to smile as she realised she was excited at the prospect of working with such a famous actress, given she had an even more famous star sleeping no more than ten metres from her right now.

Funny how quickly his job became irrelevant. At least—when they were together.

Other times, it seemed it was *all* he was. A movie star.

On set, or at Unit Base, that was who he was. Devlin Cooper, Hollywood star. Heartthrob. Sexiest man on earth. All those things.

But alone, particularly tonight, but at other times too—he was just Dev. Just a normal person. Far from perfect. The opposite of perfect, maybe.

That should be a good thing, right? That he was as normal as everybody else. As normal as her.

She sat back in her chair, stretching her legs out in front of her. It was cool, and her skin had goose pimpled where it wasn't covered by the oversized T-shirt she wore. She should really go back to bed.

She let her eyes blur, so she couldn't read the actual words of the email. But she knew them all, almost off by heart.

A request to send her CV. Such a simple thing. In this case, it was little more than going through the motions—if she wanted this job, it was hers.

And yet yesterday she hadn't sent it. Not today yet either.

Her eyes flicked to the time on the microwave. Well. Now it was tomorrow, and still she'd done nothing.

Pre-production began in three weeks, after *The Land* wrapped. The perfect amount of time to get herself sorted, maybe book herself into a hotel room for a week somewhere fun in Europe—France maybe, or Croatia—before she needed to get to London. She even knew where she'd stay—a tiny shoe-box of a room at a friend's place that she rented whenever work took her to London.

It was beyond easy. Exactly what she wanted.

She drew her legs up to her chest, wrapping her arms around herself, her chin propped where her knees touched. And just sat like that, thinking.

There was a noise, the sound of a tree branch scraping against the tin roof. It was loud in the silence, and her body jolted.

She was being ridiculous. What was she waiting for? For Dev?

Now *there* was a waste of time. He left in two weeks too, back to LA, a place where the unions could make it tricky for a foreigner to work—even if she was silly enough to daydream about things that would never happen. And that she didn't want to happen anyway.

She loved her life; it was perfect as it was. Dev just didn't fit. And as if Dev would want her to fit into his life either.

If that thought rang a little hollow she ignored it.

Instead, she leant forward in her chair, and made the few clicks necessary to reply to the email and attach her CV. Then another to press send.

She walked back to Dev's bedroom. He still slept, flat on his back now, his chest rising and falling steadily.

She'd wanted to leave, before. She wanted to leave, now.

She should, she knew.

Dev didn't need her. He had his life back on track—there was no more need for her. No more need for her to be his distraction.

Had she ever thought she was anything more?

Yes.

That was the problem. That was why she'd tried, and failed, to keep her distance.

But she wasn't about to disappear in the middle of the night.

Tonight she'd sleep in his arms—just this once.

Because, she didn't really want to leave. That was the problem.

CHAPTER THIRTEEN

THE FLASH OF blonde hair was unmistakeable.

Dev tripped, the toe of his boot catching in the uneven dirt, and he took a moment to steady himself.

'You right, mate?'

Dev nodded. A moment ago he'd been in the middle of a conversation with the young actor as they led their horses in readiness for their next scene. Now he had no idea what they'd been talking about.

He smiled. This was crazy.

He watched as Ruby flitted amongst the crew, as busy and efficient as always.

And, as always, not as much as one glance was thrown in his direction.

His smile dropped. Up until today it hadn't bothered him, her obsession with keeping their relationship private. Of course he understood.

But after last night, it just didn't sit right.

This wasn't just some fling; he knew it.

So what was it, then?

His horse shoved his head against Dev's side, rubbing his ears against his shoulder.

It yanked his attention back to what he should be doing—running through his lines.

Right now he needed to focus. Tonight, he'd talk to Ruby.

He ended up talking to her a lot earlier than that.

Dev opened his trailer door in response to angry hammering, and Ruby flew into the tiny space. She stalked straight past him, and then kept on pacing, not even catching his gaze.

'I thought we were past this?' she asked, agitation oozing from every pore.

He held up his hands in surrender. 'I have absolutely no idea what you're talking about.'

She spun about, getting right up close to him. He knew she was frustrated, but his reaction to her closeness, to the fire in her eyes, was obviously not what she'd intended.

She shoved one of his shoulders. 'This isn't funny!'

'I have no idea if it's funny or not,' he pointed out.

Ruby took a deep breath, then one big step back.

'The Australian Film Association Awards? Does that ring a bell?'

He nodded. 'Sure. Paul spoke to me about them about an hour ago.'

'And?'

'I said I'd get back to him.'

She put her hands on her hips, and just stared at him—as if that explained everything.

Ruby sighed. 'Do I seriously need to remind you about your contract? You walking the red carpet at the awards is all about generating early buzz for *The Land*.'

She then muttered something about arrogant overpaid actors under her breath.

He reached out, wrapping his hand around Ruby's. 'I said I'd get back to him. And I will—once I speak to you.'

She blinked, then glanced down at their joined hands. 'What do I have to do with it?'

He squeezed her palm, but she didn't respond. Her gaze was now wary, and he watched as she shifted her weight from foot to foot.

He grinned. 'Normally I'd hope for more enthusiasm when I'm inviting a woman to a red-carpet event.'

Her eyes narrowed. 'Is that what you're doing?'

He nodded.

'Why?'

This wasn't the reaction he'd expected when he'd had the spur-of-the-moment idea. He'd forgotten all about the awards night, but once Paul mentioned it it seemed perfect.

'Because I want you to come with me.' Then, he added, before she could say what he knew was on the tip of her tongue, 'I *want* people to know we're together.'

She tugged on his hand. Hard. He let her go, but he didn't understand why she was doing this. *He* wanted to wrap his arms around her, to kiss her. To tell her how amazing it was to realise what he had right in front of him—what he had with *her*.

But she didn't want to hear it.

Ruby wrapped her arms around herself, rubbing her fingers up and down the woollen fabric of her oversized cardigan.

'What if I don't?'

'Why wouldn't you?' he asked, slowly. Confused.

She rolled her eyes. 'I don't know, maybe because I don't want people to know about...' she threw her hands out in front of her, vaguely encompassing them both '...whatever this is.'

'What do you think this is?'

She shrugged. 'Something fun. Temporary. *Private.*'

He shook his head. 'How can you believe that? I've spent more time with you in the past few weeks than I've spent with another woman *ever.*'

He ignored yet another eye roll, his blood starting to simmer in anger. Why was she doing this? Why would she deny what they had?

'I've told you more than I've told anyone. I've revealed more of myself to you—*given* more of myself to you—than I thought I was capable of.'

More than Estelle—or anyone—had thought him capable of.

She was staring out of the window, through a tiny crack in the curtains.

'You've gone through a tough time,' she said, as if she was choosing her words carefully. 'I was just the girl who happened to be here. The distraction.'

'That's just a *word,*' he said. 'It's meaningless, and it isn't true when it comes to you—not any more. Not since that morning you came into my room prepared to bodily drag me onto set.'

She wasn't listening. 'When you go through really emotional events, it's natural to attach yourself to someone—'

'You're just making this up as you go along,' he said. 'You don't know what you're talking about.'

She crossed the trailer, putting more space between them. 'No,' she said, 'I think I do. This was never supposed to be anything serious. And it isn't.'

'Is that the issue, Ruby? *You* don't want serious, so you're ignoring what's happening right in front of you? I didn't think I wanted it either, but I can't pretend this isn't happening. I won't.'

Ruby just shook her head, still avoiding his gaze.

'You told me on the beach the other week that you learnt you didn't need anyone, years ago. I get that. I definitely get that. But I'm not like the men from your past. I won't let you down.'

Now she turned to him, her gaze suddenly sad. 'How, exactly, will you manage that?'

'To not let you down?' he repeated.

She give a sharp nod. 'Yes. What exactly have you planned for us beyond this film, and beyond this awards night?'

He was silent. Honestly, he hadn't thought beyond that. He just knew he wanted Ruby.

She smiled, very slowly. Dangerously. 'Let me guess—we'd go back to Beverly Hills.'

'I guess—' he began. It made sense, he supposed.

'And I would work where?'

He knew this wasn't leading anywhere good, but found himself helpless to change the direction of the conversation. 'I don't know. I live in Hollywood. So—'

'So that's where I'd work.'

He ran a hand through his hair. 'Damn it, Ruby—I was just inviting you to the AFAs. That's it. We don't need to plan out every second of our future together.'

'That wasn't what I was asking you to do,' Ruby said. 'Not at all.'

She walked towards him—past him—to the trailer door.

He couldn't let her leave, not like this, and in two strides he was in front of her, blocking her exit.

'Ruby, I'm new to this, too. I don't know what I'm doing.' He managed a dry laugh. 'Obviously. But—I just know that things feel *right* with you. Different right, special right. I haven't felt this good in for ever. And don't you dare attribute that to my dad.' She snapped her mouth shut. 'I can't describe it, Ruby, but I'm not ready to let it go. I can't let you walk away from this.'

She caught his gaze, her eyes a richer brown than he'd ever seen them. 'Try and describe it,' she said, so softly he leant closer to catch the words.

'Describe it?' he repeated, then, gradually—he understood what she was asking.

'Yeah,' she said. 'Describe what we have, what it is that you expect me to give up so much for—my privacy, my independence, the career I love, a lifestyle that suits me perfectly.'

Love.

That was what she was asking. Was this love?

His mind raced, whipping about in circles but coming to no meaningful conclusion. It was a word he rarely used, that he'd never said to anyone but a blood relative.

Was it even possible to love someone after so little time?

Little vignettes of their time together mish-mashed in his brain. At the beach, in bed, alone together on set, talking, laughing, loving.

He cleared his throat. 'I never said I wanted you to give up anything for me.'

She twisted the door handle, and it clicked open loudly in the heavy silence.

Then, without a word, she left.

And Dev was powerless to say the words that might bring her back.

* * *

Ruby walked briskly back to the production office, deftly handling the standard peppering of questions and minor dramas that always accompanied her progress across Unit Base.

She sounded totally normal. Totally like herself.

And why wouldn't she?

She'd known they'd reached the end of their thing. Their fling.

Fling. Yeah, that was the perfect word. Disposable.

Love.

Ruby dug her fingernails into her palms as she jogged up the steps to her office.

No, it wasn't love.

But still, it was the word she'd been waiting for him to say.

How silly, how delusional.

Besides, she should be angry with him. Angry with him for not understanding how far she'd come, and how important— how *essential*—her independence was to her. She could never give up her career, or her nomadic lifestyle. Not for anything, and certainly not for anyone.

At the doorway to her office she paused. Inside, her team were working busily away. They didn't even look up, all so used to the frantic comings and goings of the office.

Everything was just as she'd left it. As if Paul had never called her into his office, as if she'd never stormed over to Dev's trailer, and as if she'd never so vehemently refused his invitation.

And yet everything had changed. Right in the middle of all that, right in the middle of doing what she knew she'd had to do, what she'd known had been inevitable, she'd paused. For that one moment she'd reconsidered, she'd tossed everything up in the air that she'd worked so hard for, waiting on bated breath for Dev to say the words that would...

What?

Mean that she and Dev would live happily ever after?

No way. Ruby had long ago thrown away her dreams of a knight in shining armour, of the one man that would wake up in the morning and still want her—and then again the next day and for ever.

Love was for fools, for the foolish girl she'd once been.

It wasn't for her.

Dev brought the hire car to a stop in the familiar driveway.

There weren't nearly as many cars as his mum's birthday party, but there were enough to let him know he was the last to arrive. Typical—his older brothers were *always* early.

The front door was unlocked, so he followed the buzz of conversation and squeals of children to the back of the house. In the kitchen both his brothers stood at the granite bench, beers in hand, talking to his mum as she busily chopped something. Beside Brad stood a woman he didn't recognise—a girlfriend perhaps. Outside was Jared's wife who he *did* recognise from the wedding photos his mum had emailed him years ago. Two children raced across the paving on tricycles, shrieking with exuberant laughter that made him smile. But the smile fell as the adults' conversations stalled—his presence had undeniably been noted.

He strode with determined confidence to his mum and kissed her on the cheek.

Once again she looked thrilled at his appearance, as if she'd expected a no-show, or a last-minute cancellation.

Neither of which were unprecedented.

He was ashamed of his behaviour. The worst had been most recently—skipping the funeral, avoiding her calls. He'd been incapable of processing his own emotions, telling himself he'd be no use to his mum, that he'd just cause more tension, more trouble, more hassle. That his dad wouldn't have wanted him around, anyway.

Which was all total rubbish, of course.

But well before that—the decade before that—he'd neglected his mum. His visits home to Australia were limited, and always due to work, never specifically to see her. Now he suspected it was because he'd wanted to completely box away and forget his family, a family he considered unsupportive and just completely different and disassociated from him. In his family he had always felt like a square peg in a round hole.

Not that he'd done anything at all to test that theory since he was nineteen.

Or at least, not until now.

A Sunday afternoon barbecue—a simple thing, and, he hoped, a step in the right direction.

His brothers were not exactly effusive in their hellos, but they were cordial enough. Samantha, Jared's wife, and Tracey, Brad's girlfriend, were much more welcoming—if not a little star-struck, despite doing their best to hide it. It made him smile. In this kitchen, where he'd been forced to eat his vegetables and load the dishwasher, he didn't feel even the slightest bit like a movie star.

They ate lunch outside, the table piled high with barbecued everything—prawn skewers, sausages, steak, fish. Dev didn't say much, allowing the conversation to happen around him.

'I heard you're filming in New South Wales,' Samantha asked, catching his eye from across the table. Beside her, Jared eyed Dev warily.

He nodded. 'Yeah, a romantic drama, something a bit different for me.' Dev then spent a few minutes describing Lucyville, some of his co-stars, and making generic comments about how much he was enjoying working again in Australia—which, he realised as he said it, was actually true.

Beside Sam, Jared slowly relaxed before Dev's eyes.

What had Jared honestly expected him to do? Say something inappropriate? Grunt a response? Throw food across the table?

He realised he'd tensed his jaw, and that his back had become stiff and unyielding.

As Sam chatted away, asking questions about the film industry and about LA, Dev forced himself to relax.

He couldn't get angry with Jared. Or Brad.

They were just protecting his mum, and had absolutely no

reason to believe that today was the start of something new. That he wouldn't let her down—let them all down—again.

If this was a movie, the script would probably call for him to dramatically jump to his feet—to declare his grief for the loss of his father and for the loss of more than a decade of time with his family. For never meeting his niece and nephew before today. He'd use words and phrases like *a tragedy* and *regret* and *I can only hope you can forgive me* and that type of thing, and then all *would* be forgiven, and the camera would pan back, and they'd all be one big happy family. The End.

But life didn't work like that, at least not in the Cooper household.

Today was not the day for dramatic declarations, and it was not the day to expect a magic wand to be waved and for everything to be okay.

It was, and remained, simply a step in the right direction.

He needed to earn a conversation without tense undertones. And he intended to.

Ruby was the first person to tell him he was being stupid to wish the family he had away. The words had resonated more than he'd realised—when he'd been unable to sleep, when the words had been piled on top of all the other snatches of memory and guilt that filled his subconscious to the brim. Even now they still resonated, even when sleep came—mostly—much more easily.

That was a very stupid thing to say.

So to the point, so straightforward. So Ruby.

It was why he was here. She was why he was here.

'How is Ruby?' his mum asked from the head of the table, reading his mind.

'The blonde from Mum's party?' asked Brad, and Ros nodded.

'I liked her,' she said.

'Me, too,' Dev said, without thinking. Then he cleared his throat. 'She's well, I think. I don't really know—we're just colleagues. She's the Production Co-ordinator.'

As of three days ago, it was all true, but still the words felt just like a lie.

Three days since whatever had happened in his trailer. Even now he wasn't sure what had really taken place—or what he could've done to ensure a different ending. Sometimes he was angry at her, and frustrated at the crazy assumptions she'd leapt to; how unfair it had been of her to put words into his mouth, to assume the worst of him—and to fast-forward their relationship to a point where they needed to consider anything beyond the next night, or next week.

But other times he was furious with himself. Furious for letting her walk away, for not running across Unit Base—screw what anyone thought—and saying whatever he needed to say to get her to stay. Furious for not considering how she'd react, not considering what a public relationship with him might mean to her—a woman still scarred by the gossipmongering of her past. Of course she didn't want to open her life up to the world for a fleeting fling.

But would she do it for something more?

Because what they had couldn't be on her terms any more—no more secrets, no more end dates.

And she hadn't wanted to hear that, hadn't wanted to consider it.

Until *love* had come into it. Out of nowhere. And love just wasn't something he was familiar with. That he knew how to do.

The conversations around him had moved on, but he barely heard a word.

Had it been out of nowhere? *Had* it been so shocking, so unexpected?

Yes, he'd told himself.

But now—it was a no. An honest, raw, no.

Everything he'd told her in that trailer, about what he'd shared with her, what he'd revealed—that came from a place of trust, of intimacy, of connection.

A place he'd never gone before—that he hadn't been capable of going to before.

A place of *love*.

In his mother's back yard he was surrounded by his family, and he was here because of love. Love he'd tossed away, not appreciated, and now was hoping to win back, slowly and with absolutely no assumptions. It was going to take time.

And he was doing this because in his darkest moments, when the darkness had sucked the world away from him so that he was left isolated and so, so alone, *love* was what he had craved. Love from his father, but also from his family. Love and respect were all that he'd ever wanted.

In his rejection of his father, he'd tossed away a family who loved him. And they must love him, to allow him to sit here after so long.

He'd let himself believe he'd failed his father, and his family, with his chosen career.

But he'd been wrong.

His failure was in being as stubborn as his dad. For closing himself off from the possibility of love—from his family, or from anyone. He'd rejected love, because he'd been too scared to risk it—to risk failing in the eyes of someone he loved again.

Now he wanted love back in his life, regardless of the risks.

He'd wasted a huge chunk of life alone, even if he had been surrounded by people and the glitz and glamour of his career.

But enough was enough.

He wasn't letting Ruby go without a fight.

CHAPTER FOURTEEN

RUBY PADDED TO her front door in bright pink fuzzy bed socks and floral-printed pyjamas, a mug of instant noodles warming her hands.

It wasn't late, not even nine p.m., but it had been a long day and the lure of her couch had been far stronger than that of the pub and the rest of the crew.

Whoever was at the door knocked again as she opened the door just a crack, and the insistent pressure pushed the door to the limits of the short security chain.

'Settle down!' she said, 'I'm here.'

'You're not really in a position to complain, you know.' The all too familiar deep voice froze Ruby to the spot. 'I've learnt my door-knocking technique from you. Loud and…demanding.'

She ignored that.

'Why are you here?' she said, trying to sound calm. She considered, and dismissed, pretending to assume this was work-related. Or simply closing the door and walking away.

Option two had the most merit, but…well…

It was Dev. He just didn't do good things to the logical, sensible, decision-making part of her brain.

'We need to talk,' he said.

He'd stepped up right close to her door, so he could peer through the opening at Ruby. A dim globe above the door shone weak light over him, throwing his face into angular sections of darkness and light.

He met her gaze, and his was…too hard to make out.

She told herself that was why she mechanically reached upwards to close the door temporarily to unhook the chain, and then to swing it wide open and gesture him inside.

He paused for a moment, as if gathering his thoughts or taking a deep breath, and then strode into her tiny living area. He stared at her couch and its piles of blankets and magazines, and the small collection of DVDs she'd hired from the motel's surprisingly extensive supply.

Ruby swallowed her automatic apology and the compulsion to fuss and tidy. He'd just turned up uninvited—he could stand.

'So?' she asked, crossing her arms across her chest. 'Talk.'

If he was ruffled by her abruptness he revealed none of it.

'You don't have to live in Beverly Hills,' he said. 'Or work in Hollywood. I wouldn't expect you to.'

Ruby walked back to the door. 'I think you should go.'

He raised an eyebrow. 'Why did you let me in? What else did you think I was here to talk about? The film?' He laughed. 'No. You knew this was about us.'

She shook her head, but he didn't move. He just looked at her.

Now she could interpret his gaze. It was…just Dev. Honest, with not a shred of the actor's artifice that had fallen away as their time together had lengthened.

But right now, she didn't want to deal with that. She wanted to deal with the arrogant actor she'd originally thought him to be, the man who always got his way, who manipulated people—manipulated her—to get what he wanted.

As hard as she tried, she couldn't now believe any of that was true.

She didn't know what to say, but she did walk away from the door. She remained standing, more than an arm's length away from Dev, too far away to touch.

'Ruby?'

She picked a spot on the wall to stare at—a crack in the plaster beyond Dev's shoulder. 'There is no us,' she pointed out.

'There could be,' he said. 'I want there to be.'

'I don't do relationships,' she said.

'Neither do I—don't you remember?'

That night out on the main street, under the street lamp.

'We'd need to figure out the details—find a way for our careers to work together—but they can. I don't care where I live, and I don't need to cram a million films into each year.'

Ruby sniffed dismissively. 'So you'll just hang around whatever place I end up, waiting for me to come home each day from work? Right.'

He shrugged. 'Why not? I could do with a break. I've been filming back to back my whole career. And who knows? I've always been interested in production. Maybe I could look into funding a few projects, having a go at being an executive producer or something.'

Ruby tried hard to hate him for having enough money to have these choices. But couldn't.

Besides, logistics weren't the real issue. Not at all.

'No,' she said. 'This isn't what I want.'

Now she met his gaze, so he knew she wasn't talking about career decisions.

'Isn't it?' he said. He took a few steps forward. Now touching would be really easy—all she had to do was…

She curled her nails into her palms, hoping the tiny bite of pain would bring her back to her senses.

'No. I like my life. I'm happy just as I am.'

His lips quirked, and the small movement shocked her. 'Now you're just being stubborn.'

Her eyes narrowed. 'I am not. I—'

Then he was closer, really close. Still not touching, but crowding her, as he had the day they'd met.

This wasn't fair. He *knew* what he did to her, how his nearness loosened her hold on lucidity.

She felt herself faltering, felt herself tilt her chin upwards, her fingers itch to reach out and touch him, regardless of the contradictory indignation that rushed through her veins.

No. She couldn't let this happen—she couldn't let her hormones have so much control over her. She was right. She'd made the right decision to walk away. This could never end well; this was all wrong; she didn't need this; she didn't need Dev; she didn't…

'Love.'

The single world stopped the tumult in her brain. It stopped everything, actually. Ruby's whole world went perfectly still.

Automatically she opened her mouth. To what? Question? Deny?

But Dev was too quick for her.

'I figured it out today,' he said, really softly. 'That you were right. That is the word to describe this, to describe us. *Love*.'

'I never mentioned love. I don't do love.'

She sounded just as stubborn as Dev had accused her of being. She squeezed her eyes shut, trying to regroup.

She didn't know how to deal with this. How to deal with any of this.

She was tempted to repeat what she'd said before, something about the stress that Dev had experienced, about his depression, about how it was natural for him to read more into his feelings for her at such a vulnerable time.

But she couldn't say that. Firstly because she didn't believe any of it, but secondly because that neat little explanation didn't explain *her*.

It didn't explain why she'd so haphazardly and unwisely spoken in his trailer. Words she hadn't planned and a concept she didn't even know she was capable of considering.

It also didn't explain the rest. Sharing her past with Dev— not just the version she rolled out to everyone just to get it over with: her foster child upbringing, a hint of her rebellious past. But the real stuff—the stuff that mattered. The stuff that had hurt, that had changed everything—and continued to hurt.

And it didn't explain why, despite her fear of what was happening with Dev and her ingrained habit of distancing herself from men, she hadn't run away from him. Not when it counted.

So did that mean she loved him? That she was in love with Dev?

Ruby opened her eyes, incredibly slowly. She looked up at Dev, catching his gaze and holding on tight.

Did he love her? The way he was looking at her right now, it was tempting to believe it.

To imagine that finally it was actually real.

That he was her fairy-tale prince, about to carry her away into the sunset.

Away from her life as she knew it.

To her happy ever after.

That was a fantasy.

Ruby took a deep breath, and straightened her shoulders.

With great difficulty she took a step backwards, the action suddenly the hardest thing she'd ever done.

'I don't do love,' she repeated. 'This isn't love.'

Eventually, he nodded. A sharp movement.

The next thing she knew he was gone, and she was standing alone in her tiny apartment. So she walked to her kitchen, and turned on her kettle. Then, with fingers that shook only slightly, she found a new mug, and tore open a packet of noodles.

And the night continued on exactly as she'd planned.

It had to.

The Riva, Split, Croatia—two weeks later

Ruby strolled across the wide, smooth tiles that paved Split's Riva, a line of towering palm trees to her right, the Adriatic Sea to her left.

Beside her was—*Tom?* Maybe. Some guy who'd been on the walking tour of Diocletian's Palace that she'd just completed. She'd paid little attention to the tour, to be honest, and hadn't even noticed the tall, blond thirty-something guy who now walked beside her.

Accepting his invitation for an ice cream and a walk had been a reflex action. She needed to move on—needed a *distraction,* she supposed. The occasional times she did date, it was always somewhere like this—somewhere exotic and amazing where everything was light and, importantly, temporary. No hopes, no expectations.

She hadn't touched her ice cream, and it had begun to run in rivulets down the waffle cone as it melted, trickling stickily onto her hand.

The breeze whipped off the ocean, and she shivered despite the warm autumn sun.

Tom was talking about what he did back in Canada.

'I'm sorry,' she said, cutting him off mid-sentence. 'I shouldn't have accepted your invitation. I'm...' What? Getting over a break up? That didn't sound right in her head. Too...trivial. So she just finished lamely: '...not interested.'

Ouch. Quite rightly, Tom was less than impressed. He plucked her cone from her fingers, and dumped it, along with his, in a bin, before walking away.

Ruby felt a little bad, but mostly relieved. Not her proudest moment, but she just couldn't pretend any more.

This little side trip to Split for a week before pre-production began in London was *not* exactly what she needed. It was *not* the perfect distraction.

It was not helping her relax and gain some perspective and just, well...get over it.

Get over Dev.

She'd been standing looking at nothing out at the ocean, so now she turned away, heading for the small apartment she was staying in, on the second floor of a local family's stone cottage, right at the end of the Riva.

Maybe she should move her flight forward. Choosing to be alone was obviously her mistake. Surely her friend Carly wouldn't mind if she moved in a few days early? And she was fabulous at entertaining her guests. A few nights out with her and then Dev and *The Land* would all be a distant memory...

Right. Kind of like how she'd told herself that working for Dev for another week wouldn't be so bad, even though she'd then spent every hour of her work day preventing herself from throwing herself at him and babbling something ridiculous about having made a terrible mistake…

It had been most frustrating. She had done the right thing. For her.

She didn't need Dev. She'd been absolutely happy before she'd met him. She didn't need Dev to make her life complete, to give her anything in life she wasn't perfectly capable of achieving herself. Her life was full and lovely and gorgeous—and she didn't need a partner, and certainly not a husband, to finish it off.

And she'd hate herself if she ever let herself believe differently.

It wasn't peak tourist season in Croatia, and so around her people dotted the Riva, rather than cramming it full. Some were obviously tourists—couples holding hands, families with small crowds of children. Others not so much. An older couple walking in companionable silence, a group of women chatting enthusiastically away.

I wish Dev were here.

The thought came out of the blue, and Ruby walked faster, as if to escape her traitorous subconscious.

The thing was, now wasn't the first time she'd wished such a thing.

Like on the plane to Heathrow, where one of the movies was so awful she'd turned in her seat to list all its flaws before realising that it was a stranger snoring softly beside her, and not Dev.

Or waking up in her gorgeous little Split apartment, the sun flooding through gossamer curtains onto her bed, and she'd turned and reached out for familiar, strong, warm, male skin.

But all she'd touched was emptiness.

She really needed to get over this.

She'd never spent every night with a guy like that—never in her whole life. That had been her mistake. She'd got too used to him, and now he was like a habit. A bad habit.

That theory didn't even begin to convince her.

Ruby undid the latch of the wrought-iron gate that opened to the series of stone steps leading to her apartment.

As she unearthed her keys from her handbag she remembered her sticky ice-creamy fingers, tacky against the smooth metal.

What a waste of a perfectly delicious ice cream.

The random thought made her smile, but she noticed that something was blurring her vision.

Not tears, at least, not proper ones. These stayed contained within her lashes. Mostly.

In the bathroom she washed away the remnants of vanilla and caramel, and made the mistake of meeting her own gaze.

She looked pale, and blotchy—but mostly just miserable.

Like a woman who'd just walked away from the love of her life.

And who had absolutely no idea what to do next.

The sleek, low-slung car slid to a stop at the end of the long red carpet.

It was still daylight—late afternoon actually. Dev bit back a sigh—these awards nights started early and went notoriously late. He could think of another billion or so places he'd rather be right now.

Outside, temporary metal fencing kept rows of fans a good distance away, but he could already hear them calling his name. Other cars arrived around him, and women in dresses every colour of the rainbow emerged into the sunlight in front of the glamorous, sprawling Darling Harbour hotel. Their partners in monotonous black provided little more than a neutral backdrop.

Dev watched as each couple walked only a few metres before television cameras and shiny presenters swooped. Dev knew the drill; he'd been here—or at events just like this one—a thousand times. He knew this stuff, knew the name of the designer of his suit, exactly the right thing to say and how to smile enthusiastically for every single fan's photo.

He could do this.

Graeme twisted in his driver's seat to look over his shoulder at Dev. Graeme, Dev had decided, was his new Sydney driver. He was a good guy—and he still hadn't breathed a word of his and Ruby's relationship. In this industry, such loyalty was very nearly unprecedented.

'Ready?' he asked.

Dev shook his head, but Graeme was already climbing out of his seat. 'I'll just be a minute,' he said. Not that another minute would make him look forward to the next handful of hours any more.

Besides, he was perfectly capable of opening his own door.

But—it was too late, and he straightened his shoulders, and brushed imaginary lint off his extremely sharp designer suit.

He could do this, he repeated, looking towards the red carpet, and the many ascending steps it richly covered.

Then the other door opened—the door across from him, facing the street—and he twisted around, surprised.

'Graeme, you may need a bit more practise opening—' he began, but the words stuck in his throat as a woman slid onto the leather seat beside him, and Graeme shut the door firmly behind her.

Ruby.

'Hi,' she said, very softly.

She wore a long dress in red—a deeper red than the carpet—a red that matched her name. It flowed over her body, slinky in all the right places, and with a V neckline that was…remarkable.

Her blonde hair was perfectly sleek, her make-up immaculate, her lips—of course—ruby red. It was Hollywood glamour—red-carpet glamour.

'Hi,' he managed, although it took quite a bit of concentration.

Her lips curved into a smile, but it was only fleeting. She caught his gaze with hers, and didn't look away.

Her gaze might have been rock steady, but uncertainty was obvious in her chocolate eyes, in her shallow breathing, and her fingers that twisted themselves in the delicate fabric of her dress.

'I thought that if I was with you, that if I *needed* you…' she took a deep breath '…that I would lose myself.'

He nodded, knowing now was not the time to speak.

'I used to confuse sex with intimacy, and I've worked really hard not to make that mistake again. And I haven't. But now I've made a different one—I've confused intimacy with just sex. A fling. It's taken me a few weeks to figure that one out.'

He could see the depth of emotion in her eyes, and he desperately wanted to move closer—to reach out—to touch her. But he didn't move. He needed to let her finish.

'I tried to ignore it, even when it was happening. I tried to pretend that I didn't care, that I didn't worry about you more than I can remember worrying about anyone—ever. I kept a distance between us, I closed my eyes and pretended you weren't hurting, because then I wouldn't need to admit that I hurt, too. For you.'

And for herself, too.

'I'm not familiar with love, you know?' Now she looked away, but only for a moment. 'I don't know how to recognise it—how to filter it out from my ancient habits—to distinguish it from misguided infatuation or fantastical daydreams. But when I wasn't with you, when I walked away from you—that didn't make it easier. What I felt didn't go away, not even a little bit. What I was feeling for you ruined *everything*.'

But she was smiling, and he realised he was smiling, too.

'I don't want this, you know?' She nodded out of the door, towards the hordes of people and the observant cameramen who were trying to peer through the black tinted windows. 'But I didn't want this even without the movie-star thing. Even if you worked in Props, or wrote scripts, or didn't even work in film at all.'

'Me either,' he said. 'I thought I was good at going it alone. That I had it all sorted, the best way to live my life.'

'Me too!' she agreed, and laughed briefly. 'And it's risky changing direction.'

'What if I decide this way is better? Then what happens if it doesn't work out?'

Ruby nodded, her eyes widening in surprise. 'Exactly. It's scary.'

Dev shrugged. 'I decided it was worth the risk.'

And it was. Even when she'd said no, it had still been worth it. Even though it had sucked. Really, really sucked.

His life wasn't going to be about regrets any longer. Except—even then, when he'd laid his heart on the line—he hadn't been entirely an open book. He'd still withheld one thing.

'I love you, Ruby Bell.'

Quick as a flash, she replied, 'I love you too, Devlin Cooper.'

Then for long moments they smiled huge, idiotic grins at each other.

Over her shoulder a camera flash momentarily stole his attention, bringing him abruptly back to reality—to *his* reality.

'What about the paparazzi, Ruby? The gossip and the rumours? With me, it's as good as guaranteed.'

She shocked him when she shrugged. 'I used to think that I had to prove something to the gossips—prove them right or prove them wrong. But you know what? I don't care any more. You arrived on set amidst a storm of rumours, and you didn't change one thing—you didn't react, you didn't engage, you didn't deny. You were just you.' She paused, then reached out to grip his hand. 'People can say whatever they like about me, or you, or us—but I know the truth. We do. And I've decided that's all that matters. I'm in control of my life, no one else.'

She was amazing. If he hadn't fallen long ago, just that would've pushed him over the edge.

'Do you want to walk the red carpet with me, Ruby?'

She nodded, and amongst a sea of camera flashes he opened his door, and stepped out, only to turn and offer her his hand.

She slid across the seats, and swung her gold stiletto heels onto the red carpet. He bent closer to whisper in her ear.

'This is serious, you know that? For ever stuff. Happy every after, like in the movies.'

'No,' she said, so firmly he went still. He caught her gaze as she looked up at him from the car's leather interior. 'Not like in the movies,' she said, 'and not like in fairy tales.'

Finally she reached out to take his hand, letting him pull her to her feet.

They stood together, side by side, the red carpet before them, fans screaming, cameras as good as shoved in their faces. But all he was aware of was Ruby, of her hand in his, and the look in her eyes as she looked up at him. With love, and with everything she had to give.

He knew he was looking at her in exactly the same way.

'This is real life,' she said.

* * * * *

Mills & Boon® Hardback

March 2013

ROMANCE

Playing the Dutiful Wife	Carol Marinelli
The Fallen Greek Bride	Jane Porter
A Scandal, a Secret, a Baby	Sharon Kendrick
The Notorious Gabriel Diaz	Cathy Williams
A Reputation For Revenge	Jennie Lucas
Captive in the Spotlight	Annie West
Taming the Last Acosta	Susan Stephens
Island of Secrets	Robyn Donald
The Taming of a Wild Child	Kimberly Lang
First Time For Everything	Aimee Carson
Guardian to the Heiress	Margaret Way
Little Cowgirl on His Doorstep	Donna Alward
Mission: Soldier to Daddy	Soraya Lane
Winning Back His Wife	Melissa McClone
The Guy To Be Seen With	Fiona Harper
Why Resist a Rebel?	Leah Ashton
Sydney Harbour Hospital: Evie's Bombshell	Amy Andrews
The Prince Who Charmed Her	Fiona McArthur

MEDICAL

NYC Angels: Redeeming The Playboy	Carol Marinelli
NYC Angels: Heiress's Baby Scandal	Janice Lynn
St Piran's: The Wedding!	Alison Roberts
His Hidden American Beauty	Connie Cox

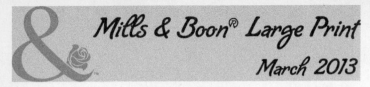

Mills & Boon® Large Print
March 2013

ROMANCE

HISTORICAL

MEDICAL

Mills & Boon® Hardback
April 2013

ROMANCE

Master of her Virtue	Miranda Lee
The Cost of her Innocence	Jacqueline Baird
A Taste of the Forbidden	Carole Mortimer
Count Valieri's Prisoner	Sara Craven
The Merciless Travis Wilde	Sandra Marton
A Game with One Winner	Lynn Raye Harris
Heir to a Desert Legacy	Maisey Yates
The Sinful Art of Revenge	Maya Blake
Marriage in Name Only?	Anne Oliver
Waking Up Married	Mira Lyn Kelly
Sparks Fly with the Billionaire	Marion Lennox
A Daddy for Her Sons	Raye Morgan
Along Came Twins…	Rebecca Winters
An Accidental Family	Ami Weaver
A Date with a Bollywood Star	Riya Lakhani
The Proposal Plan	Charlotte Phillips
Their Most Forbidden Fling	Melanie Milburne
The Last Doctor She Should Ever Date	Louisa George

MEDICAL

NYC Angels: Unmasking Dr Serious	Laura Iding
NYC Angels: The Wallflower's Secret	Susan Carlisle
Cinderella of Harley Street	Anne Fraser
You, Me and a Family	Sue MacKay

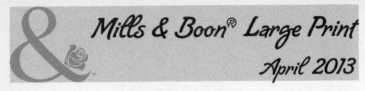

Mills & Boon® Large Print
April 2013

ROMANCE

A Ring to Secure His Heir	Lynne Graham
What His Money Can't Hide	Maggie Cox
Woman in a Sheikh's World	Sarah Morgan
At Dante's Service	Chantelle Shaw
The English Lord's Secret Son	Margaret Way
The Secret That Changed Everything	Lucy Gordon
The Cattleman's Special Delivery	Barbara Hannay
Her Man in Manhattan	Trish Wylie
At His Majesty's Request	Maisey Yates
Breaking the Greek's Rules	Anne McAllister
The Ruthless Caleb Wilde	Sandra Marton

HISTORICAL

Some Like It Wicked	Carole Mortimer
Born to Scandal	Diane Gaston
Beneath the Major's Scars	Sarah Mallory
Warriors in Winter	Michelle Willingham
A Stranger's Touch	Anne Herries

MEDICAL

A Socialite's Christmas Wish	Lucy Clark
Redeeming Dr Riccardi	Leah Martyn
The Family Who Made Him Whole	Jennifer Taylor
The Doctor Meets Her Match	Annie Claydon
The Doctor's Lost-and-Found Heart	Dianne Drake
The Man Who Wouldn't Marry	Tina Beckett

0313 GEN STD LP